THE
WATCHERS

THE
WATCHERS

Jane Louise Curry

Atheneum   1975   New York

FOR MARY AND CHIP

—AND THE CATS, OF COURSE

Map and drawings on pages 124, 134, 144, and
157 by Trina Shart Hyman

Library of Congress Cataloging
in Publication Data

Curry, Jane Louise.   The watchers.
"A Margaret K. McElderry book."
SUMMARY: Rebellious and unhappy at being
shipped off to live with strange kinfolk
in the mountains of West Virginia, a young
boy is drawn into an ancient conflict
that moves back and forth in time.
[1. Space and time—Fiction. 2. Mountain Life—
Fiction] I. Hyman, Trina Schart. II. Title.
PZ7.C936Wat   [Fic]   75-8582
ISBN 0-689-50030-0

Published simultaneously in Canada by
McClelland & Stewart, Ltd.
Manufactured in the United States of America
Printed by Sentry Press, New York
Bound by The Book Press,
Brattleboro, Vermont
Designed by Suzanne Haldane
First Edition

THE WATCHERS

Exile

It began to snow. May first, spring along the Ohio, and up here it could still snow. "Uh! Old Winter's got a little kick left in her yet," the mailman observed, as he switched on the windshield wipers. "Like my old lady."

Young Ray Siler's thin nose seemed to grow even sharper as he allowed himself a sour smile and a comforting surge of contempt that included the mailman, his Jeepster, and the world in general. They were all conspirators in shipping him off to Uncle Durham and Aunt Star. Every mile of the way up to Moars' Corners deepened that bitterness: shipped into the hills like a parcel nobody else would take. The world was shrunk to—to snow and cornball humor and overheated air and smelly cartons of day-old chicks.

Ray's eyes slid from his snowy window to the red-faced driver. It was illegal to give rides in government vehicles, wasn't it? He considered writing an anonymous letter to the main post office up in Charleston to report "repeated violations" but after a moment gave it up as impractical. If his father changed his mind and let him come home, he just might need an illegal U.S. Postal Service ride back down to Willocks.

The car swung around a curve so tightly that the chicks were tilted into heaps and set up a wild peeping in their perforated boxes. "Sorry, friends," the mailman said over his shoulder. "My fault. But you get off at the next stop along with Mister Siler here, so you ain't got long to suffer." He swung into a left-handed turn without easing off the gas and neatly floated up around the right-hand curve that followed. In the next short straight stretch he eyed the sullen, pinch-faced boy beside him. Not a flicker. Looked as if he wouldn't bat an eyelash if the Jeepster drove right off the side of the mountain.

Ray wasn't grieving for his home upstate. He didn't give two hoots for Apple Lock. But he did care about the why and how and where of his going. He had been close to tears when the big Greyhound bus eased out onto Front Street and took Route 2 south out of Apple Lock, because nothing—not reason, sweet-talk, rage, pleading, hitting Aura Lee with the meat platter, or

black, weeping despair—had made his father turn a
hair, let alone change his mind. Ray was to go to his
mother's kin down in Withers County.

He had to go because Aura Lee had two children of
her own, and when she married Ray's father she meant
to be a good mother to his little ones, Joe and Alva, but
she wasn't about to take on a strapping thirteen-year-old
troublemaker who idolized his dead mother and hated
Aura Lee from her platform shoes to her real mink eyelashes. If that was the way she felt, it was fine with Ray.
But after he begged to go to one of his older brothers
and tried to find one who would take him, he began to
feel a bit like a basketball: dribbled in circles, handed
off, dribbled aimlessly, and handed off again. Dan's
wife Susie was epileptic—not bad, but she had her
hands full with the twins. Marv and Charlene had an
extra room, but they'd been married only three months,
and Marv hemmed and hawed until Ray saw it was
hopeless. Wally had had an apartment in Weirton, but
when he was laid off at the steel mill for such "gross
and persistent absenteeism" that even the shop steward
said he had it coming, he let it go and joined the army.
"Wisht I could take you along down to Fort Campbell,
Ray boy. I surely do," said Wally, secure in the knowledge that he couldn't.

The closest Ray got to sympathy was Charlene's
"But none of you even *know* them Withers County
Clarks, do you?" His gratitude shriveled at the edges
when she added pensively, "They must be good folks to
take on one more when they got four of their own."

There wasn't even a last-minute chance to run away, to take a bus for New Orleans or Los Angeles, because soft-hearted Charlene came into town on the orange bus with him, and hung around the terminal until his Greyhound left, buying him *Sports Illustrated* and a Hank Aaron special edition, and six Zag-Nut bars, which she liked and he didn't.

The Greyhound pulled into Charleston late in the afternoon, and after two foot-long hotdogs and a strawberry milkshake, Ray checked at the information desk for the bus that stopped at Mozart on the West Virginia Turnpike. The information lady pronounced it "Mozzert" and said he just had time to catch it at gate three. From Mozart the eight-o'clock Munsie Mountain Coach took him to Taggert, where he'd been met by the Reverend Mr. Maclehose (brother to the mailman), who was an old friend of Dan and Susie's preacher up in Apple Lock. Handed off again. Maclehose to Maclehose to . . .

At the Corners, a short, stout man, in shirtsleeves despite the snow, came out of Moars' Store, bellowing, "Late again, Mac! Five whole minutes." He leaned in at the open window. "Like to see you come in late tomorrow when you're bringin' them county checks."

Maclehose grinned. "Fat chance. All them good voters'd go lean on Judge Dishart, he'd go lean on the postmaster, and that'd be the end of yours truly. Flat as a cow-pat from all that leanin'. Here, Arbie, I brung you some live ones. The two hundred chicks are C.O.D., but the kid's for free. Name's Ray Siler, goin' up Twillys'

Green Hollow. My brother collected him off the bus at Taggert and put him up last night. Brung him up to Willocks after breakfast."

Mr. Moar's red-faced grin blurred itself into a formal heartiness, a face so smooth and different he might have peeled the first one off. "Well, now. Welcome to Moars' Corners, Ray boy. We weren't lookin' for you till tomorrow, but sooner's better, like they say You got a suitcase there? Take it along inside. We'll see about gettin' you up to the Hollow after a bit."

As Ray, dismissed, carried his ancient duffle bag up the wooden steps, Mr. Moar was saying, "How *is* the good Preacher Maclehose? Got a lot bigger congregation down there in Taggert, I reckon. Say, how much I owe you on these chicks? They must've upped the price on me again. I know I sent a check."

"Only four eighty-five, Arbie. That's right. Here's a dime. Wait a minute, now. I got a nickel here somewheres." The mailman's voice dropped a note. "Say, that kid don't look much like them queer Twillys' Green folks. You can tell them a mile off. How come he's . . ."

Ray shouldered the door open and let it slam behind him.

Inside, Moars' Store was a big box of a room awash with fluorescent light and Loretta Lynn singing at top volume over the speaker system. One wall was lined with freezers and coolers, and the floor was laid out in a maze of jam-packed shelves. A faded blonde woman and a dark, skinny girl in blue aprons embroidered across the bib with YOU GET MORE AT MOARS' lounged at the two check-out stands near the door. The woman smoked a cigarette with quick, nervous puffs, and the girl sipped a bottle of Dr. Pepper through a lipsticky straw. There wasn't a customer in sight.

"Can I help you, honey?" The blonde woman peered at Ray nervously, as if she wouldn't know what to do if he said yes. "The soft drinks is clear down by the back wall," she volunteered hopefully.

It wasn't a bad idea. Lunch already seemed an age ago. "Can I leave this somewheres?" Ray swung the duffle bag off his shoulder. SILER, it read in faded stenciled letters, S/4 101 AIRBORNE.

"Sure, any old where." She flipped a hand toward a pen full of the biggest shopping carts Ray had ever seen. "Park it in one of them."

"That's right, Ray boy." Mr. Moar backed in through the front door with two of the chick cartons and set them down on the first checkout counter.

"You look like your stummick's as empty as my wallet, boy. You pick yourself out something and see you get a couple of them cream-filled cakes for dessert. On the house." He chuckled. "On Arbie Moar, that is. That's 'R. B.' for Russell Boyd. And this here's Missis Moar, Jessie to you." He indicated the blonde woman, who smiled jerkily. "And this other's Miss Bonnie Yanto. This is Ray Siler, Bonnie, that cousin of yours, come early."

"No cousin of mine," Bonnie said flatly. The blue eyes above the sharp cheekbones were bored. Pale makeup over a dark skin made her blank little face even more masklike. Her hair was ratted up into a lacquered beehive, with one long lock springing out at the back to hang like a dark waterfall between her shoulder blades. She shrugged. "He can come along up the Hollow with me, though. I don't mind quittin' early. There's nothin' to do here oncet the mail's sorted."

Moar clucked reprovingly. "Don't you go telling me he's no cousin of yours. Isn't he Dream's sister's boy? And aren't all you Twillys' Green folk kin? Why, if you set out to draw your fam'ly trees, it'd look like one big rats' nest. It's the same over in Hoop Hollow, where Jessie's from, only they aren't so stand-offish."

Bonnie only shrugged her shoulders and sucked up the last of her Dr. Pepper.

Mr. Moar, with a jerk of his head, drew Ray off behind a small mountain of syrup in gallon cans. As he laid a pudgy hand on the boy's shoulder, his face made one of its abrupt shifts, seeming almost to lengthen and draw leaner as the eyes widened and twinkled and the mouth pursed up to whisper. "You keep your eyes open up there, Ray boy. There's folk—college professors and the like—who'd like to know any little thing about Twillys' Green, old songs, queer ideas, whatever. How long they been there, where they come from. 'Place of Mystery,' one of them eastern newspaper writers called it when he couldn't get an elbow in the door. You find out what they do with themselves up there, Ray boy, and it might just be worth a little something. O.K.?"

Ray, bewildered and not a little alarmed, muttered something about being hungry and edged off toward the nearest aisle. It did not go straight through to the back, but beyond the instant coffee and teabags zigged to the left and deposited him midway along a stretch of cookies and crackers of every imaginable shape and flavor. From the pretzels he zagged into the tinned vegetables and arrived at the soft drinks, having navigated by fixing his eye on a wall poster of a pretty skier holding out a bottle over the caption *It's the Real Thing.* There was such a variety that it took a while to make up his mind: colas, root beers, red pop, cherry and strawberry sodas, juice-drink, sugar-free, and the same assortment in purple for grape and blackberry. There were brands he'd never heard of, like Purple Lightning and Mountain Maid. There was a bank of six-packs of every kind of orange and another of lemon and lime and things like Sprite and Seven-Up. But there were more colas than anything.

In the end Ray settled on a bottle of Red Lightning and picked up a bag of corn chips on his way to the bakery shelves, where choice wasn't so much of a problem. There were donuts, and a bunch of boxed pies that looked mostly crust, but three-fourths of the section were taken up with puffy plastic-bagged sandwich bread and great heaps of snack cakes. Ray took two of the cream-filled ones.

"That'll be fifty-two cents." Bonnie poked at the register keys as if she expected an electric shock when the bell rang.

"But—" Ray's ears burned as the flush came up from under his collar to spill across his cheeks. "Mister Moar said . . ."

"He said have those cream cakes on him, not all of it."
Under her breath she added, "Catch him givin' away
more'n five-cents-wholesale-worth a week!"

Ray counted his change out onto the counter. When
the last penny was added, it came to forty-two cents. "It's
all I got," he said stiffly. "But my Dad sent some more
in a money order to my uncle. I'll bring it tomorrow out
of that.

"No credit," Bonnie said impassively, one finger
hooked in the cash drawer. Mrs. Moar looked like a
distressed sheep under her frizz of blonde hair—sympathetic, but concerned about the sheepdog, who had
disappeared with the chicks into the stockroom.

"I'll take the corn chips back." Ray reached for the
packet.

As if that were the cue she had been waiting for,
Bonnie swept the coins into her hand. "No need. I can
loan you a dime." She pulled a white plastic handbag
from under the counter, found a dime, and shoved the
drawer shut. "Don't you get crumbs all over the place,
now."

The snow had stopped. There was even a gleam of
pale sunshine, so Ray took the corn chips and cakes
outside to eat on the porch. The chips were good, but
the sickly-sweet imitation-cream filling in the soft cakes
turned his stomach, which had been none too steady to
start with. Just what sort of hole was it he'd been shipped
off to? Only the stiff-necked Clark pride he'd learned
from his ma kept him from asking. He went back in for
the red pop he'd left half-drunk on the counter and
saw Bonnie flip something suspiciously like a crumpled

drinking straw into the waste basket. Sneaking a bit of interest on his dime. They watched each other like unfriendly cats, pointedly uninterested.

Arbie Moar appeared in the stockroom doorway. "Two letters for Twillys' Green today, Bonnie. You stick 'em in your reticule there, and you'n the boy can take off now. Come in early tomorrow if you want to make up the time. I made a good deal last week on a load of wheat off a wrecked 'semi' and I got to run down to the feed mill in Willocks in the morning to pick up the flour. Jessie could use a hand clearin' out a place for forty-fifty sacks."

As Bonnie shrugged herself into her coat, he added casually, "Almost forgot. You tell Aunt Mavee I could let her have some of them chicks I got in for Lew Boddie." He carefully straightened the hand-lettered sign that read SPECIAL SAVING—Sirup by the Gallon—ONLY $3.95. I hear tell a fox got her rooster the other night."

"If I see her." Bonnie tied a pink chiffon scarf over her hairdo. The way she said it, Ray wondered whether she were laughing at Mr. Moar, but her face was still like a window with the blinds down.

Bonnie, mini-coated and thinly booted, climbed the rutted road at a half-trot, intent on keeping warm. Ray, in his hand-me-down hunting jacket, heavy cords, and new boots, was sweating after the first half-mile. The duffle bag felt a pound heavier with every hundred yards. Though below, where the road was open to the sky, the thin snow had melted, half an hour of steady climbing had brought them into a winding gully nobody in his right mind would call a road, where the overhanging hills shut out the sun. The stony, rutted trace was treacherous with snow.

Just over three miles up—Ray thought it a good four, but the most he was used to was a quarter-mile hike out to the school bus—they came to a wide place, a pause in the old road before it flung itself up the last steep and stony hill. Off to one side a stripped and gutted old Studebaker rotted in a cocoon of briars. Seven battered mailboxes fastened on a single board were propped against the post they once had sat on.

"How come the mailboxes and no mailman?" Ray stopped to catch his wind.

Bonnie gave a breathy little snort. "Mr. Moar, he's the substation, and he gets money to pay old Mutch Boddie and his horse to take letters 'round the hollows, but soon's I started work down to the store, he give me the Twillys' Green stuff. My pa reckons he cut Mutch's pay down and keeps the difference."

Ray nodded at the boxes, which read in faded letters, *Tullo, Yanto, Mattick, Lillico, Clewarek.* "What kind of wacko names are those? Italian?" He hoisted the duffle bag to his shoulder again. "Where's *Clark*? I don't see any Clarks."

Bonnie gave him a scornful look. "You don't know nothing, do you? There's been Yantos and Tullos in Twillys' Green since the Year One, I guess. And there *ain't* any Clarks. It's Clewarek. Aunt Star and Uncle

Dream and the kids is Clewareks, like your ma was."
She had begun to shiver in her too-short coat but made
no move to go on. Her little painted face worked, and
she spat out the words in a hoarse whisper as if she
hated Ray for being there to say them to: *"Like your ma
was before she got away.* I'm going to get away too,
but don't you go telling. I nearly got enough money,
and when I get to Nashville my name's gonna be
Bonnie Sue Anderson, and I'm gonna sing on the
radio and TV." She looked alarmingly near tears. "If you
tell anybody, I'll say you lie, you hear? I'll—I'll say you
stole them corn crisps down to the store." With that
parting shot she turned on her heel and climbed the
hill at a half-run.

Ray followed in stumbling confusion. Ray *Clewarek*
Siler? And Bonnie called Uncle Durham "Uncle Dream."
That was weird. And there was Mailman Maclehose's
crack about being able to tell Twillys' Green folk a mile
off. If it were true, ugly Bonnie didn't promise much for
the rest of them.

But Ma was one of them. Sure, her hair had been
dark at the roots when she put off bleaching it, and she
looked sun-brown even in winter, but she was *pretty*.

His old world lost behind him, Ray plunged and
slithered up the stony track in a deepening dread of the
new one. His mother had never talked of the Hollow,
never told funny or tall tales of her childhood as his pa
had of his; and of her kinfolk, all she had ever said was
that they were "close." Thinking back and shamed not to

know, Ray wondered if there had always been a bitter-sad edge to her sweetness. Close? There were other closes than loving ones. Close-mouthed. Close-fisted. Take your pick.

He slipped and the duffle bag slid down to wedge against a tree trunk. Scrambling after it, Ray suddenly froze where he crouched. Along the thickly-wooded slope opposite, across the gully from the shoulder where the road climbed, a low shadow, dark against the snow, skimmed the hillside. For a moment it kept pace abreast the hurrying Bonnie, then faded back and was lost in the trees. It took up again, an elusive mote in the corner of the eye, as Ray came to his feet and raced for the hill's crest.

The Hollow

Just over the crest of the hill, the road and the creek
that spilled down-gully crossed paths at the point where
a stout wooden bridge spanned the spillway of a small
pond. It might once have harbored trout but now held
only an echo of the dark trees and leaden sky. Fifty
yards along the wooded gap the snow turned to slush
and then to mud; the hills drew back, and the rising
valley opened out. One branch of the creek ran down
from a lesser gully, straight ahead, but the main branch
curved down from the right, a swift, deep-banked
wriggle of a stream cutting down the middle of the
Hollow.

In the Hollow, the sun had already melted the last of the snow. The spring-green hills that shaped the little valley were naked of trees as far as their crests, but there giant hemlocks towered, and beeches. The muddy yellow slopes were bearded with corn-stubble, and here and there scrub and briars fenced in a broken apple tree. Barbed wire sagged from post to tree to privy to post around vegetable patches where old squash vines rotted and dried-out tomato plants hung from their stakes.

Seven cabins with ramshackle sheds for barns straggled down the long creek-side. Two were log houses, the rest gray weather-worn plank, roofed with oak "shake" shingles, and all but the topmost with drooping porches, barking dogs, and plumes of chimney smoke. The house at the head of the hollow gaped eyeless and toothless, its windows shattered, its porch posts and doors long ago burnt up in black iron stoves.

It was worse than bad. The shadow in the woods forgotten, Ray hugged the Hollow's awfulness to him with a bitter satisfaction. The worse it was, the more his dad would have to answer for, the more it would take to make it up. He'd write to Charlene first—a long letter with pencil drawings of weedy yards and weedier hillbillies—and swear her to secrecy. The rest would get dutiful postcards and feel pleased with themselves until Charlene spilled the truth, which she was bound to do. But the letter to Charlene would have to wait until he had a good list of horrors. Ugliness and privies weren't enough. The Siler house in the hills up back of

Apple Lock had got its indoor plumbing only six or seven years back, and Dan's wife Susie—her idea of beauty was a graveled yard with an iron umbrella-tree thing to hang pots of plastic geraniums from.

Where the road petered out, a rattletrap old Ford pickup with a wired-on Chevy grille and no fenders hunched in the lee of a clump of willows. Beyond, a muddy track led to a footbridge over the creek and a path up across the stubblefield to the nearest house. Bonnie waited until Ray was across and, with a toss of her long lock, said he'd better keep close behind if he cared about the state of his hide.

Ten yards on, Ray saw what she meant. The big gray dog on the first porch left off barking to come barrelling down the field, snarling and flashing his fangs even after Bonnie's handbag caught him a sharp clip on the jaw.

"You git *down*, you flea-bit monster! Patches, *down*! You too, Rose, you git on out of here," she shrieked, as Patches was joined by a galloping yellow hound. Grabbing Ray's hand, she dragged him toward the house. "Mer-rull!" she yelled. "Call off your dog!"

A boy in jeans and a faded sweat shirt appeared on the porch. "Who you got there?" he called and, without waiting for an answer, bellowed, "Ma, here comes Bon with some kid." Bonnie and Ray and their escort gained the porch before the boy, who looked about fourteen or fifteen, waded in to haul Patches off by the scruff of his neck. "You shut your noise, dog, hear?"

Patches sat down obediently and grinned. Yellow Rose, the excitement over, trotted back up the creek.

"Who's that? It's not Lissy's Ray, is it?" A neat, angular woman in a plaid wool shirt worn over a flower-print dress, appeared in the cabin door, wiping her hands on a flour-sacking apron. "I declare, it *is*! Roney?" She turned to yell into the house. "It's Lissy's Ray."

To Ray she said, "Lordy, and us all thinking it was tomorrow! Well, it don't matter one little bit." She planted a big kiss on his forehead and folded him in a floury, bony hug. "Welcome home, child."

She held him out at arm's length for a good look. "Oh, yes. You're mostly your daddy, I reckon, but I can see Lissy in those blue eyes." She smiled as a tall, stooped man in overalls appeared at her side. "Ray, this here's your Cousin Roney. I'm your Cousin Faye. Leastways we're second cousins, a time or two removed. But just 'Faye' and 'Roney' is easier. Bonnie you know, and that's our Merle."

"I'm right glad to meet you, Ray," said Roney, sticking out a hand as big as a middling ham. His lank hair, like his wife's and son's, was dark, almost black, and like the others he had the dark skin that seemed all the darker for the pale blue eyes and long, bony face.

His voice was as gentle as his big hand. "Merle, you go pass the word up to Opal's and across the creek. Opal can send Sue Ellen up to Star and Dream's, and on up to Uncle Penn and Aunt Mavee's. Sue Ellen's faster'n you."

It was like falling into a feather bed. No amount of determination on Ray's part could have shut out the unexpected warmth. Once he had been treated to a glass of goats' milk (which was, oddly, refreshing and revolting at the same time), and after Bonnie had been sent to the kitchen pump "to wash off that downhill face," the Yantos and Ray headed for the little cluster of houses midway up the valley. Old Uncle Roy and Aunt Bessie Tullo came down from their little hillside-perched house to their nephew Adney's where Adney and Opal and their Sue Ellen and Sue Ellen's two-year-old waited on the sagging front porch. The Matticks—Harry and Luce and their son—crossed the creek by way of a bouncing plank, bringing a gallon glass jug of applejack. Cousin Opal brought out a platter of plump sourmilk cookies and glasses for the women and children. There was a pretty, unchipped one for Ray with daisies around it. "This'n's for you, because I recollect how particular your mama always was," said Opal. The men drank straight from the jug.

The welcome-party snowballed noisily as it rolled uphill, moving back across the creek with the Matticks to gather up Aunt Erla and Uncle Cloyce Lillico and their three young grandchildren. While white-haired Aunt Erla urged coffee and gingerbread all around, Uncle Cloyce passed a squat brown jug around the little circle of men.

Merle poked Ray in the ribs. "Ask for a taste," he whispered, and doubled up laughing when Ray did and had to spray most of it right out again. Brother Wally had once paid Ray a trick like that up home in Apple Lock with a flask of white turpentine and got a chipped tooth in return. This time, after he managed to stop choking, Ray passed it off with a feeble grin. The men all laughed again and turned back to their talk.

Merle's grin, unlike Wally's crow of triumph, was an offer of shared glee. "That's white lightnin'. Old Arbie Moar sells it out his back door on dark nights. Uncle Cloyce dumps it in his old cider jug so's Aunt Erla can use the Mason jar." Merle snickered happily. "Kind of separates us boys from the men, like they say, don't it?"

Ray wiped his mouth with the back of his hand and tried hard to sound as easy and friendly as the older boy. "Man, you could strip off floor varnish with that stuff! How come they got any insides left?" No one was looking, so he rinsed the taste out with the last of his coffee and dumped the dregs into a straggly barberry bush beside the porch steps.

At least the warm moonshine glow in his stomach steadied it against the bucking of the plank bridge when Uncle Cloyce headed everyone back across the creek and up toward the Clewarek cabin. Aunt Star came hurrying down the muddy path to meet them, Uncle Dream ambling after. On the porch of the log house Rainelle, June Ann, Mary-Mary, two-year-old Jody, and a spotted dog hung back shyly.

Aunt Star cried and gave Ray an awkward hug—awkward because she was clearly a good ways along toward having a new baby—and Uncle Dream just held Ray's hand hard in his two big ones, saying simply, "Our Jimmy Bob would've been just your age if the Lord hadn't took him when he was little. This house has need of you, Ray."

The Clewarek house was larger and more solidly built than the others and was apparently the Hollow's gathering-place. The downstairs room was cleared, the chairs and hulking old television set were pushed against the wall, and an enormous trestle table grew down the middle as planks and sawhorses were handed in at the front door with a speed that told of practice. Aunt Star and Uncle Dream's bed was stood on its end in a corner to make more room, and its feather mattress handed up into the loft.

While the women bustled in and out and the jug made the rounds on the porch, Uncle Dream asked Ray about Wally and Marv and Dan and Alva and Joe, about what their new step-ma was like, and about "our Lissy's passing on." Ray could no more get used to the "Lissy" than the Clewarek. His father had always shortened his mother's name Melissa to "Milly." Now, somehow, under this long, bony uncle's gentle questions, Ray found himself telling about his mother's pain, about the operation put off until too late because his pa mistrusted doctors.

"Sounds a hard man." Old Uncle Roy Tullo shook his head.

"Mebbe he didn't used to be. Mebbe it was that Korean war," Harry Mattick said, rubbing a hand over his stubble of gray beard. His eye wandered to where his lanky son Delano crouched by a bare rose bush and stroked the spotted dog. "He might've been different when Lissy met him down to Kentucky. War does that. Hardens up some men's hearts and breaks others."

Delano, or Delly as Merle had called him when he told
Ray about it, was only three months out of the VA
Hospital over at Beckley, where he'd spent more than a
year off and on.

The girls had all the while been running in and out,
bringing heavy baskets and napkin-covered dishes. Ray,
pretty much talked-out, was relieved when he and
Merle were drafted to bring up more benches and
chairs. Aunt Erla's eight-year-old grandson Bob-White
and Delly Mattick were dispatched up the track at the
head of the Hollow to the Dreegos, to give Sue Ellen
and young June Ann a hand with the seemingly end-
less outpouring of jugs and jars.

"I don't know what we'd do without Aunt Mavee,"
sighed a breathless Aunt Star, shutting the firebox on the
stove and dropping the scoop back in the coal scuttle.
"Faye and Opal and Luce and me, we counted on doin'
some shopping down to Moars' tomorrow when the
welfare checks come in. Seems the last day or two 'fore
they come, we're always down to biscuits and bacon
grease."

She passed a handful of cutlery to Rainelle and
stepped back so Ray could shove the last bench in
place. "That's fine, Ray honey. Anyhow, like I was
saying, it's a real pot-luck stew tonight—all our scraps.
But Aunt Mavee's sendin' down a lot of her special
good things, so we'll have us a treat after all."

"I couldn't do all she does." Bonnie's mother sighed,
spooning drop-biscuits into a blackened pan. "She is the
strongest old lady. Seems she never gets wore out."

Cousin Faye, like Bonnie, was too thin; but where her daughter was wiry and abrupt, she was slow-moving and had wilted visibly as the afternoon wore on.

They all *talked* such a lot. Ray had got used to the long silences of people who have nothing to say to each other, and now the unaccustomed talk made him nervous. Even his mother's friendship had few words to it. They just understood each other. With no prying or tinkering. This cheerful, unhurried chatter of women and low murmur of talk from the men on the porch was like the slow, sweet droning of a carnival snake-charmer's flute. It tempted you to stretch and yawn and sprawl your legs out on the broken-backed sofa, and Ray set his mind against it like a wary half-wild dog.

Aunt Mavee Dreego came down at six to take command of the deep stewpot, adding herbs and applejack and chunks of smoked pork and venison. A tall, bony old lady with gray hair still streaked with black, she could have been anything from sixty-five to eighty. It was impossible to guess.

At seven, when everyone had gathered, she sat herself at the foot of the table and Uncle Penn Dreego at the head. While Uncle Penn intoned, "We thank'ee Lord fer the bounty of yer hills, the shelter of yer valleys, and the gift of our Lissy's boy here," Ray, at the old man's right hand, was eyeing the twenty-five bowed heads uneasily. A gift, was he? To these odd, dark-skinned folk? With their high cheekbones and queer washed-out blue eyes circled with shadows like smudges

of walnut stain, it was no wonder outsiders thought
them peculiar.

As Uncle Penn prayed on, Ray found four-year-old
Mary-Mary Clewarek staring at him. He had not
noticed before, but her eyes alone were black and
oddly close together. Her mouth hung slackly open, but
as Ray crossed his eyes at her, the answering squeal
sliced across Uncle Penn's blessing.

" 'Gain! Do i'gain!" Mary-Mary demanded excitedly
in a thick, blurred voice.

"Amen," Uncle Penn pronounced loudly, making a
ferocious face that left Mary-Mary wide-eyed with fear
and delight. "She ain't right in the head," the old man
confided in a whisper to Ray that must have reached to
the far end of the table. "A sweet, lovin' little gal, but
she gits in a swivet at the least thing. Best pay no attention."

Eyes twinkled all the way down the table, and the
three Lillico grandchildren giggled helplessly. "Ma'y-
Ma'y's silly," piped two-year-old Red.

Mary-Mary ignored them. Unexpectedly she swung
her arm up to point over Ray's shoulder. Her mug of
cider spilled onto her plate and slopped down the front
of her dress. "Zee! I zee man!"

"A man, honey?" Aunt Star dabbed at the mess with
her apron. "Sure, we got lots of men. Uncle Penn and
Daddy and Uncle Harry. Lots of them."

But that was not what Mary-Mary meant. For while
everyone else passed biscuits and side dishes and tucked
into the stew, Ray, twisting toward the window, met the

thoughtful gaze of a man, a shadow in the dusk that gathered early under the steep hills. A moment, and he was gone.

For the fragment of a second that the light from the window fell on the man, Ray glimpsed a face as strange and terrifyingly familiar as something seen deep in a dream: long hair shining blue-black as a crow's wing, cold silver-pale eyes, and a heavy gold collar as broad as a man's hand.

Rainelle

"That man—who was he? He . . ." Ray stopped. Every-one was smiling.

"She sees things, too," Aunt Star murmured. "Things that ain't there. Best to just smile and nod. It don't mean nothing."

Ray stared. "But I saw him too. A long-haired guy. He looked a lot like"— Ray flushed—"like all of you."

The smiles faded. The children were as still as small rabbits puzzling at a new scent. Their elders looked either bewildered or faintly offended, almost as if they thought he was mocking the little girl. Only old Aunt

Mavee seemed unrattled. Her sharp glance skewered Ray as if she could see right into his head with it.

"I guess I imagined him," Ray mumbled, backing down. "Maybe it was a shadow."

Uncle Penn cleared his throat and clanked his knife against his enamel cup. "No sense lettin' good food git cold. Pass some of that side meat here."

The command brought a relieved burst of talk and a clatter of plates. The stew meat—a mixture of pork "side meat," venison, chicken, rabbit, and something unidentifiable that Ray afterward learned was 'possum —was passed around a second time, the gravy following it in a chipped green pitcher. Shared out among twenty-six, it came to only a forkful or two apiece, but there was plenty of pale gravy and more than enough biscuits to sop it up with.

The oven was kept busy with drop-biscuits all through the meal, and one big saucepan was filled again and again with sauerkraut from the five-gallon crock Delly had lugged down from Dreegos'. The Mason jars of Aunt Mavee's corn relish, watermelon pickles, and ginger applesauce made the rounds until a good dozen stood empty by the front door. The hum of talk dried up completely in the concentration on serious eating.

The children washed their last bites down with cider while their elders emptied the big speckled enamel coffeepot. After the plates were wiped clean with a last bit of biscuit, out came the pies. They had been nestling in the stove's warming closets up above the cooking surface where the saucepans sat: pumpkin and sweet potato and apple. Somehow, in between all the

gossip and to-ing and fro-ing, Aunt Mavee's sacks of
dried apples and pumpkin and sweet potatoes had been
soaked and boiled up, the pastry had got mixed and
rolled out, and the pies had been baked in ovens around
the Hollow and then brought up to keep warm in
Star's stove. With their pie, the children had more cider,
and for the others Uncle Penn dragged a squat stone-
ware jug out from under his chair and sent it around
the empty coffee cups.

"Metheglum," he said with a wink, pouring Ray a
very small tot that slid down sweet and cool and then
began to glow. "That's honey wine the way my granddaddy made it, and his granddaddy afore him."

Roney Yanto pushed back his chair and stuck out his
long legs. "Where's your guitar, Rainelle honey? How
about we have a little music?"

Rainelle ducked her head shyly. She looked plead-
ingly at her father. "Do I got to, Daddy?" She was about
Ray's age and pretty in her own odd way, with long
reddish hair much lighter than most in the Hollow.
Her eyes were a woods-violet blue, sometimes vacant,
sometimes, like now, vague and anxious.

"You go upstairs and get it, honey," Uncle Dream
said. "What's a party 'thout music?"

With the plates scraped and stacked, everybody
pitched in to take the long table apart and draw the
chairs and benches into a wide horseshoe around the
fireplace. While Merle and Bob-White refilled the coal
buckets from the bin on the front porch and Uncle
Dream got the fire going, Ray slipped out the back door

to lean dizzily against the rough log wall. Two days of junky snack-meals and misery, topped off with too much heavy food and such a confusion of people, well, it was like . . . like being inside a dream.

That man now. Why should they say there was no man when there *was*? And someone had followed him (or, at least, followed Bonnie) up from Moars' Corners, or had he imagined that too? Ray sat down on the edge of the little back stoop and put his head between his knees to stop its swimming.

Several minutes later, perhaps five, a cold nose touched Ray's ankle and he jerked awake just in time to keep from toppling off the porch. The little spotted bitch whined and cocked her head quizzically.

Uncle Dream was hunkered down beside him. "You want a glass of water?" he asked simply. "Little bit of bakin' soda in it, mebbe?"

Ray nodded dumbly, and in a moment June Ann, the one between Rainelle and Mary-Mary, was there holding out a glass of cloudy water.

"Daddy says you just come in when you feel like it," June Ann said. She slipped away, leaving the door open a crack.

Inside, the children's voices sang out in a raucous challenge: *"Hoop snake, hoop snake, head for your hole!"* followed by Rainelle warning in a gruff little voice, with a riffling of strings:

> *I got me a great big hickory stick*
> *And a little piece of coal.*

"Hoop snake, hoop snake, bite your tail!" shrieked the little ones, and Rainelle threatened,

If you don't roll away right quick,
I'll hang you on a nail.

Hoop snake, hoop snake, quick now, roll!
Or I'll pin you down with this old stick
And stuff your mouth with coal.

Hoop snake, hoop snake, poor old son!
The day a hoop snake can't hoop up,
His running days are done!

Rainelle was really good. She didn't just strum a lot of chords for harmony, the way brother Wally did so showily, but picked a running melody with little flirts and quirks. She was, astonishingly, better than some Ray had heard on Porter Wagoner's show on WSTV. He eased the door open and slipped in to sit against the wall and listen while Uncle Roy Tullo and Cousin Adney Tullo sang an old round about a blue tick and a bear with Rainelle coming in third, coaxing dog-howls and bear-grumbles out of the old Sears guitar until the round wound down into a storm of clapping and a chorus of "Do 'Along Down Home'," and "Let's have 'Runnin' on the Mountain'," and "How about one of them old riddle-songs?"

Rainelle brushed a damp lock of hair from her eyes, tucking it behind her ear, and shook her fingering hand as if it were a dust mop. "Just one more. I ain't played in a good while, and it gets kinda numb."

"How about Sue Ellen's song?" Bonnie asked. It was the first word she'd said in hours.

"You made up a song, Sue Ellen?" Opal looked at her daughter in surprise.

"Let's hear it," commanded Aunt Mavee. "It's a long whiles since we've had a new song."

Rainelle hesitated. "I dunno . . ."

Sue Ellen hugged her little boy close. "I don't mind," she said mildly. "But Bonnie'll have to sing it. I sure can't."

Ray settled back with a hand over his mouth to hide his grin. But whatever he'd expected after sharp-faced Bonnie's outburst on the hill about going down to Nashville to be a singer, it wasn't what he heard. A hard country twang or maybe rockabilly, he thought, but not this sweet, rich, simple sadness. *"In Greenbrier Hollow,"* Bonnie sang,

> *In Greenbrier Hollow*
> *When the briers bloomed in spring,*
> *My love said "Follow, for if you will,*
> *I'll weave you a sweet-grass ring."*
>
> *When cloudberries flowered,*
> *"Come climb up top," he said,*
> *"Where the moon that rides up the Hollow*
> *Won't spy our sweet-grass bed."*
>
> *But that Board called him up*
> *While the berries was a-growin',*
> *Sent him off to war to die—*
> *The why's beyond all knowin'.*

Now I got me a little boy
To keep the dark nights warm,
A berry-brown boy to nestle in
The hollow of my arm.

But there's none to stroke my hair,
O, none what knows the art
To warm the winter's chill away
From the hollow of my heart.

No one said a word for a minute or two after the lament died to a whispered echo of the last phrase from Rainelle, hunched over her strings. Bonnie leaned back against the TV, quiet, almost pretty in the fire-glow. Sue Ellen just rocked Sweet William back and forth and studied the floor. Ray wanted to clap, but he sensed something moving behind all those fire-flickered faces that he did not understand.

Aunt Luce Mattick was first to break the silence. "Mebbe you'll write it down for me when you get home, Sue Ellen, honey?" she asked softly. Sue Ellen nodded and smiled down at Sweet William, fast asleep.

Uncle Harry tucked Aunt Luce's hand in his and gave it a squeeze. "Time to go home," he said. "Cloyce? The babies is asleep, and little Red there's gonter topple over any minute. How about I carry him down fer y'? Delly c'n bring Dawn. She looks like the sandman give her an eyeful too."

Rainelle, June Ann, and Mary-Mary went up the loft ladder first, with Aunt Star coming awkwardly behind.

By the time Ray followed, the girls had already slipped into shapeless nightgowns and then into the big low double bed at the end of the loft, next to the chimney-warm wall. Aunt Star pulled shut a curtain made from two old cotton blankets, and by the dim light of the naked fifteen-watt bulb, showed Ray his bed by the little window at the opposite end. He had it to himself, since Jody was still little enough to sleep downstairs in the old hand-carved crib.

"I put an extra quilt on for y'," Aunt Star said, as she turned down the covers, "because I know you ain't used to our mountain nights. Come summer it gets awful hot up here, but the kids sleep out in the rockhouse then. There, now. It's a good soft bed, and I hope you sleep good."

"Aunt Star?" Ray whispered, as she pulled the light-string and turned toward the ladder-well. "That song . . ."

"Weren't it good?" Aunt Star gripped the handrail nailed to the wall beside the ladder-well and felt for her footing. "But it must've been hard for poor Sue Ellen. It was about her and Frank Mattick, you see, Delly's twin brother. He got killed out there in Vietnam after that cease-fire."

It wasn't what Ray had meant to ask, but it silenced him. He had meant to ask whether anybody had a tape recorder, because a song like that, sung like that, ought to sell, ought to make a lot of money. A silly question anyway. Who in the Hollow would have a tape recorder? And who would have thought a song, a made thing, would be about real people and secret feelings?

Downstairs, Aunt Star let out a gasping laugh and could be heard to murmur to Uncle Dream, "I think them steps and me have had it for a while!" Then everything was quiet.

The bed was good. And soft. But it sagged a bit in the middle. Ray had got into the habit of sleeping on his stomach, and for that it just wouldn't work. The pillow, fresh-covered but smelling of chicken feathers, hit the floor first thing. After a restless half hour he pushed himself up to sit propped against the head of the bedstead.

He was debating whether the *Sports Illustrated* article on "Yesterday's Heroes: Where Are They Now?" would be worth digging down to the bottom of the duffle bag for his flashlight so he could read it when his eye was caught by a gleam in the darkness outside. Drawing his feet under him, he raised up on his knees and pressed his face against a windowpane.

The light came from a few yards up-Hollow from the house and only a little below the level of the sleeping loft: a thin yellow thread of light as tall as a man, or taller. There was no other cabin up that way. It was, in fact, where the hill ought to be. Where the hill *was*. As Ray watched, the thread widened to a ribbon, spilling light down a stone-stepped path; and then the door— for it was a door—opened wide upon a shallow firelit room and a slender figure silhouetted in its frame.

Ray had been holding his breath and now let it out in a sigh of nervous relief. The rockhouse. It must be the rockhouse, where the girls slept in the summertime.

The word had meant nothing to him when Aunt Star spoke it, but it clearly would be just such a hollow under an overhanging rock ledge, built out like a lean-to and given a proper door. Both Indians and the early settlers had used such houses, he recalled. But why no windows? As stuffy for summer sleeping as any loft, he would have thought.

The girl in the doorway turned to speak to someone inside, and as she moved, Ray saw her face plainly. It was Rainelle. Rainelle wearing some sort of embroidered cloak, and her hair in two long plaits. More peculiar goings-on. Ray eased the window sash up an inch in hopes of hearing who she was talking to but couldn't make out a word. *Ah claygooroway zarall zarallint deeksat*, it sounded like. Just nonsense. He strained to push the sash higher, but stopped as it gave a wooden groan of protest. Shrinking back, he held his breath as Rainelle moved out to look upward. Starlight glinted in her eyes.

"Ssst!"

Ray whirled away from the window.

Rainelle.

Rainelle stood shivering in her white muslin nightshift, her hair hanging down every which-a-way, peering at him nearsightedly through the gap in the blanket curtain.

"It gits stuck when it's damp," she whispered. "It'll take the both of us if you want it clear up."

Outside, the rockhouse door sagged on one hinge, and its frame opened not onto shifting firelight, but into darkness.

Under the Hill

The first thing Ray did the next morning, after an early
breakfast of oatmeal porridge washed down with thin,
milky coffee, was to head for the rockhouse that crowded
under the high hillside. He had tossed half the night,
at first wondering whether he had been seeing things
and finally deciding in a tangle of bedcovers and resentment that the Twillys' Greeners had to be hiding something. Maybe a clutch of halfwit cousins, grownup
Mary-Marys; or some bank-robbing kin lying low. Or a
moonshine still. The strangers had to be family. You
could tell that by looking at them.

The rockhouse was empty.

It was not only empty, but alarmingly different. The window—he didn't recall there being a window last night. "Hi, anyone there?" he called. When there was no answer, he eased carefully past the sagging door into the shallow room.

It was not the same room. There was no fire circle in the center of the floor; only a rickety little table. Three rusty iron cots without mattresses crowded along the walls. Ray shivered. The air was dank and chill, and where the low ceiling of the little cave curved down to become the back wall, moisture dripped from the bare rock. The floorboards there were sodden, and even in the center of the room they were damp to the touch.

Floorboards? Ray looked around him wildly. Last night there had been no flooring, only the earth and a circle of stones around the fire he'd glimpsed behind the girl. Turning in a whirl of confusion, Ray pushed out through the door. The bottom hinge gave a protesting *screak*! as another nail pulled loose.

Crossing the stony ground to the little porch at the rear of the Clewarek cabin, Ray hoisted himself up to sit, legs dangling, on the edge. He felt, in his confusion, almost as sick as he had the night before when Uncle Dream came out to offer him the soda water. What did it all mean? What kind of hole had he been stuck in?

Ray sat there for a good ten minutes wishing he were anywhere else in the world before it occurred to him that it was Thursday. A school day. And there he sat. Inside, he could hear Aunt Star talking to June Ann over the clink of dishes in the dishpan. Ray looked at his watch. Eight o'clock. The school bus couldn't come much beyond Moars' Corners, and to catch it, there had to be a good half-hour's downhill hike. Suddenly anxious, he jumped down and headed around the cabin.

Halfway around, it struck him as funny. You'd think he liked school! But it wasn't that. He had a queer, smothered feeling that the Hollow had closed in around him, and that the Outside was steadily, stealthily drawing away. He needed to grab hold of *some*thing familiar.

Uncle Dream sat on the lid of the front-porch coal bin, his feet propped on an upended apple crate, his back against the log wall. He wore a frayed and grimy baseball cap pulled down over his eyes.

"Naw, no use your goin' down by yourself 'thout Rainelle or June Ann to kind of show you the ropes," he said to Ray's question. "Be too late for the school bus anyhow. You been on the go for two days. Likely you can use a little rest." He yawned. "School'll still be there come Monday. Star don't like June Ann goin' all that long ride if she's sickenin' with a cold."

It was true that June Ann had appeared at breakfast a little droopy-eyed and sniffled once or twice. Right off, Aunt Star had begun to cluck over her as if she were flat out with the flu. Why all the fuss, seeing that every one of the children at dinner the night before had been equally pasty-faced and runny-nosed, Ray did not understand.

"What's the matter with Rainelle? Or did she already go?"

"Rainelle?" Uncle Dream looked around vaguely. "Rainelle, she didn't sleep too good last night. She come down at the crack of dawn and took off somewheres. Up Top, mebbe."

Ray supposed he ought to be pleased at not having to go to school. He was impressed that his uncle should think it no great matter, but he remained uneasy. "I got this note from the principal up home," he said reluctantly. "What if it's got the date on it? The principal in at Willocks, he'll know when I got here."

More to the point, it would be a bad start when the note quite probably included a copy of the Apple Lock truant officer's summary report on Raymond Clark Siler: *Uncooperative and uncommunicative, though not openly defiant or troublesome. Unreliable. Unexcused whole or part-day absences for school year 1974–75 to date: 39.* What the principal had added to that, Ray could imagine. *Raymond consistently under-performs, not from a lack of ability, but because he seems totally unmotivated. Dental and medical reports indicate that he is quite healthy. The boy's father is unable to offer any explanation.* Etcetera. Too bad he hadn't lost the letter altogether.

Uncle Dream, tilted back with his eyes still shut, considered. "I don't see as you need worry. Now and again Star runs into one of them teachers down to Moars' and they say how bad it is we don't see the young'uns get in every day, but I can't see as how it hurts much. They say you can't get a good job 'thout schoolin', but they ain't work for *any*body these days. There's young Delly. He went right through high school and learnt a lot about motors and all in the army, but he can't get work no more'n me. Oh, oncet in a while Roney and Ad and me, we can pick up a day's work, but . . ."

"What's that I hear?" Aunt Star appeared around the corner of the house with a tin can full of water for the rose bush, which looked as if it might, with a little encouragement, put out a few leaves. With a wink at Ray, she drawled, "You want a day's work? How about filling that coal bin up again, so's I won't run out in the middle of supper. I don't suppose Erla'd say no to a couple of buckets neither. Takes half the day for Cloyce to fetch her any when his back's troublin' him."

Uncle Dream stretched. "I don't mind. Long as Ray's here to give me a hand, we might as well carry some up to Dreegos' too. I seen Aunt Mavee busy goin' up and down with her old pack basket yesterday morning. She hadn't ought to do that."

Star smiled as she poured the water in the little hollow around the bush. "How come? Because a woman's bad luck in a mine? Leastways she's got the sense t' take hers off the coal face and don't go robbing the pillars like lazy Dream Clewarek."

Uncle Dream explained about "robbing the pillars" as he and Ray climbed to the mine entrance, a natural cave in the hillside across the creek and up from the Clewarek house. It was the practice of taking coal from the thick "pillars" left to serve as supports for the great weight of the hills overhead. Like commercial mines, the Hole, as the Hollow called it, consisted of several parallel galleries connected at regular intervals by cross-passages. The pillars consisted of the unmined coal between these passages. In worked-out mines, such pillars held the last coal left, and scavengers risked the danger of rockfalls and collapsing ceilings.

Twillys' Green had kept the Hole to itself, however, and it was in no danger of being worked out. The seam was in some places as much as seven feet thick and probably underlay the whole of the ridge. It had been mined since time out of mind, but there was plenty of coal without robbing the pillars. Not, Uncle Dream admitted, that he hadn't done it once in a while when Star was in a hurry for a scuttle of coal.

The mouth of the cave, half-hidden by shrubs and tall grass and the thorny shadow of a thickly-branched old crabapple tree, was no higher than Uncle Dream's breastbone. Entering meant stooping and shuffling awkwardly forward until the cave opened out around them. Once in, Ray saw pickaxes, shovels with splintered handles, battered buckets, broken lanterns, all tumbled in heaps against the walls. The dim light came in part from the opening through which they had entered and partly through a smoke-blackened shaft that pierced the roof to show, far above, a scrap of blue.

Uncle Dream dragged a battered once-red child's wagon from behind a stack of crates and lifted one crate into the wagon bed. Then, rooting among the buckets and lanterns, he came up with two old-fashioned miner's hats with carbide lamps attached.

"Here, this ought to fit you, boy. Hold on a minute till I light it." He set the grimy cap on Ray's head, and from a hip pocket produced a metal "safety" spark-maker. He squeezed the handle once to be sure the flint sparked against the metal rasp and reached up to light Ray's lamp and then his own.

Turning, Ray saw the blurred beam from his lamp sweep across the rough walls. The cave looked only fifteen to twenty feet deep, but at the back, what once had been a deep and narrow crevice angling into the heart of the hill, had been widened to make a passage into the first gallery of the Hole. The sloping floor of the passage, barely wide enough for the wagon, was worn smooth from use, and the walls had a raw and fractured look. Apparently blasting powder had been used to widen them—without much care for the shape of the results. A great heap of chunks and shards had been cleared into an out-of-the-way corner.

Uncle Dream smiled at Ray's wary fascination. "You never been underground before. I reckon a mine is kind of ordinary, but caves now, they can be homely and eerie all at once. Lookit there. Could be an Indian did that, or even the first Dreegos that come over the Gap." He touched a finger to the rock of the chamber wall close to the crudely widened crevice.

Bending down, Ray saw a shallow carving: a double-lined circle. At first he thought it nothing more than that, but on closer inspection an eye and a faint pattern of scales showed it to be a snake with its tail in its mouth. He grinned, looking up to meet Uncle Dream's smile. "I guess it's a hoop snake, like in Rainelle's song. But there isn't *really* such a thing, is there?"

Uncle Dream's look of surprise made him look more

awake than Ray had seen him yet. "Hoop snakes? Lordy, yes! Don't you have 'em up north?"

"No-o." Ray was cautious. "Have *you* ever seen one?"

Uncle Dream rubbed his dark stubble of beard thoughtfully. "No, but that don't mean nothing. There's lots of things I ain't seen. I ain't seen the ocean or Paris, France, but that don't mean they ain't out there. My granddaddy—your great-granddaddy, that would be—he near caught a hoop snake oncet. You see, they give a sorta *whip!* with their tails to set 'em rollin, and then they grab aholt of the pointy tails with their mouth. Grandpa, he come within a inch of snaggin' this one before it rolled away. I reckon most everybody round here's seen one or knows somebody who has. Arbie Moar, he grew up down in Kentucky, and they got 'em down there too."

It still sounded far-fetched, but there wasn't much point in arguing about it. Ray moved so that the glow from his lamp swept upward. Halfway to the ceiling, the shallow lines of another shape caught the light. "That one there looks sort of like a hand." Palm up, it suggested a warning as clearly as if the peculiar squiggles across it had read *STOP*.

"Um." Uncle Dream wasn't one to pretend an interest he did not feel. "You'll have t'ask Uncle Penn about that. He drew a picture-copy of all sorts of them scratches years ago, before this hole was made wider and a lot of 'em got spoilt." He frowned. "Look here, this mine's kind of a Twillys' Greeners' secret, so don't you go talk about it round outsiders. No point in lettin' wasps know there's honey about. All right? Now, you come along and stick close. The Hole ain't big, but it's plenty big enough to get lost in. We'll keep to the right on the way in. That wall's kind of a rock dike, so there's no side galleries off it." His voice at the last was muffled as he disappeared into the mountain with the red wagon clattering behind.

There had been good reason to fear the wasps getting at the honey, as Uncle Dream put it. As he explained later, the tale of mining in the nearby hollows was an equally sad one and, sadly, not uncommon. Back in the 1880s, scouts for the big eastern iron works had come through West Virginia and Kentucky, buying up hundreds of thousands of acres of mineral rights—not the land itself but the buried minerals under it. The unsuspecting hill folk were paid fifty cents an acre for their treasure. Time passed, railroads snaked up the main river valleys, iron and steel boomed, and grandsons who never knew their grandfathers had sold the earth under their land met the coal men, come to claim the riches they had bought for pennies.

What with Twillys' Green Hollow being up back of beyond, and the Twillys' Greeners having kept so much to themselves, the coal buyers who came through Withers County seemed to have missed them altogether. Others had not been so fortunate. With strip-mining, farmers, dirt-poor to start with, were left with useless shale heaps and streams as bitter as their hearts. It had happened as close as Sour Creek, and in Moon

Hollow, where there was a deep mine, things were hardly better.

Not that Twillys' Green Hollow hadn't been changed by it all. It had been a world to itself, with neat little tree-lapped farms "Up Top" and the now-derelict house down in the Hollow watching over the stock in the grassy meadow. The hills and hollow fed them well and clothed them, and they mistrusted the outside world just as it resented them for their odd looks and the mystery of their being there at all. Nevertheless, Twillys' Green was changed beyond recovery.

Old Man Yanto, Roney's dad, and the young Cloyce Lillico signed up one day for work in the Moon Hollow mine, thinking they might spend a day or two a week at it—"just enough to buy the young'uns boots fer winter, seeing as Uncle Gunnet weren't alive to make 'em any more." But the work was five days a week or nothing, and the money was never enough. If you had no time to plough and plant or hunt or tend stock, you had to fall back on the store at the Corners (then only a shack with shelves) for pork and flour and cornmeal. While you were at it, you tried—and got a taste for—potato chips, Ritz crackers, red pop, and penny candy. Inevitably, the county school board discovered the Hollow and decreed that the children had to go to school.

Within a few years, every family except the Dreegos had been drawn the first step away from the land. Eventually, the ridge-top farms, knee-high in grass and invaded by groundhogs and field mice, were abandoned for new cabins along the creek, built with bought lumber and wired for lights and washing machines. Electricity lines had followed the narrow road up to the Hollow.

"There was hard times after Moon Mine shut down in 'forty-eight." Uncle Dream panted as he swung the pick. "Uncle Ez Lillico, he died. Always was weak-lunged, and the coal dust did for him. What they call 'black lung' now. Aunt Runa, she didn't outlast him by much. Just as well. She didn't have nothin' but a piece of wore-out land when he was gone. No widow's pension atall." He stopped to mop at his sweaty neck with a bandanna.

"It weren't a union mine till right at the last. The coal company, they'd fire anybody seen even pass the time of day with an organizer, so the UMW never got a foot in the door until forty-eight. That was when Big Tom Yunnie from Horse took a whole shift crew, Cloyce and Roney and Uncle Roy among 'em, down to a union organization meeting in Willocks. They let on they was goin' to the races at Kentinnia Downs and come back as UMWA Local 7890. The company, they grit their teeth and signed the contract. It wasn't much skin off their teeth by then. They closed down two months later. It was bad times for the coal business."

Ray tipped a last shovelful of coal into the crate on the wagon. He couldn't have cared less about the Hollow's ups and downs, but until he had figured a way to get out and home again, it wouldn't pay to put his uncle's back up by saying so. "How come that aunt didn't get a widow's pension?" he asked. "If her old man joined the union, I mean." The question came automatically, but it was the darkness, the sense of being-out-of-the-worldness that held Ray's mind. The damp, still blackness beyond the lamps' glow oppressed him.

Uncle Dream headed back for the cavern-opening with Ray steadying the wagon's load from the rear. "It don't work that way," Uncle Dream said. "For a pension you had to work twenty year to start with, five of 'em after forty-six for a union operator. Nobody at Moon mine had a look-in, seeing they closed down in forty-eight." He ducked his head where several thick wooden beams, held in place by stout props, supported a weakened area of the rock ceiling overlying the coal seam. "Watch your head there now."

Suddenly, cold, dark water seeped through the stitching of one cheap suede boot, soaking Ray's sock. He squelched on for several yards, then let go the crate. "I stepped right in a puddle," he called after his uncle. "I got to wring my sock out." Leaning against a coal pillar, he bent down to unlace the boot.

Uncle Dream's light dwindled to a firefly down the corridor. "Keep right where you are," his echoing call came back. "I'll dump this load and come for another." His light winked out.

Left alone at the edge of his own dim island of light, Ray felt suddenly cold. Colder even than last night when Rainelle had given him such a fright. Rainelle. He had meant to find her, to ask how she did it. There had

to be a secret way in and out of the loft: a ladder outside, a trap window, something. She had really had him
going, thinking there were two of her. He refused to
think about the mysterious fire and the unexpected
window. When he shivered, he told himself it was the
cool air after the sweaty work.

The silence began to be alarming. Ray lifted the foot
in the wet boot to retie the lace, and a bit of coal that
crunched under his other heel crackled loudly, the
sound lingering in the still corridors not like an echo, re-
peating, but as a fading presence. His own breath
seemed noisy, the only sound left under the mountain.
The more softly he tried to breathe, listening for his
uncle's returning footfalls, the more loudly the blood
thrummed in his ears. It was some minutes before he
became aware of another sound beyond that soft, swish-
ing *thrum*. It was water. Not a stream, not even a trickle,
but the silvery seeping whisper of walls breathing water.

"Uncle Dream?" The call came out thinly. "That
you?"

Something—a presence in the darkness that was more
than earth and water—touched him more sharply than
the cold.

"Uncle Dream?" He ventured it more loudly this
time. He daren't move for fear of getting turned
around—if he weren't already. It was a dirty trick to
leave and not come right back. More resentful than
frightened, Ray hugged himself and jiggled up and
down, trying to shut his ears to the sigh and rustle of
the dark.

And that dark grew. At first it seemed illusion, a trick of the eyes; but when Ray kept still, holding the lamp on his cap steady, there was no mistaking. The darkness sucked softly at the light glinting on the rough wall opposite and glimmering in the black dust on the floor, dimming it, closing in around it, pressing toward its center. Ray's heart thumped painfully, and his resentment was swept up into a sudden flood of hatred that spread, unreasoning, across his mind like a sheet of black water.

A silly name, Dream. And all that crazy talk about how it was better before they got money. . . . How come they didn't go back to the old ways if they were so good? That had to be a load of rubbish. Slowly, unwillingly, he felt himself drawn away from the pillar's shelter toward the rough stone wall across the gallery. Fingers tingling, he touched both hands to it and found it unaccountably warm and smooth. Dry, too, like silk against his palm, alive and not-alive. . .

"Yo!" Uncle Dream's call abruptly shattered the darkness. "Comin' in!"

Ray shuddered with relief and turned back to lean weakly against the great pillar. As his uncle's lamp bobbed nearer, his own seemed to brighten, its pool widening across the floor.

"What's the matter, boy? Y' look white as a sheet. You see a rat or just a bogey?" Uncle Dream grinned.

"You—you were gone so long," Ray mumbled.

"No such a thing." Uncle Dream's big hand closed on Ray's shoulder reassuringly. "No more'n two-three minutes."

Ray stiffened, biting back an angry denial. Two or three minutes? It must have been a good half hour. He looked at the watch Susie, Dan's wife, had got with Top Value stamps for his going-away, and his bewilderment deepened. According to it, no more than half an hour had passed since they first stepped inside the outer cavern.

"The place does kind of get to y'," Uncle Dream acknowledged kindly. "I reckon there's no need to go all the way back into the face. We'll just shave us off a crateful here and be out in a minute. This here's drier anyhow."

He hefted the pick and ran his eye along the thirty-foot thick pillar. There were a number of uneven spots where he could chip off sizeable amounts. Ray followed with the wagon, tossing the larger lumps in and shoveling up the smaller.

The crate was almost full when Uncle Dream, undercutting a projecting lump, swung the pick more vigorously than he had intended, biting deep into the pillar. "Back off," he warned Ray. "This whole chunk could come down."

He next gingerly chipped out a long cut about a foot above his undercutting and then knocked off the coal between the two cuts. Just as he bent to heft the largest piece into the wagon, the pillar gave a sort of groan, and a great triangular weight of coal broke loose, slumping downward to crash into rubble and fill the air with coal dust.

"Cover your face!" Uncle Dream croaked through the cloud. "And don't move."

When the air had cleared a little, Ray saw him, cap-less, black with grime, sprawled on the floor, his legs buried under a weight of coal.

"Lord be praised," he croaked. "It's a wonder the old Hole didn't go up like a bomb with that much coal dust floatin' around. I got to clean that stuff out one of these days. Anyhow, there's no bones broke, I reckon." He sat up and dragged his legs free. "But Star's like to break my head. Mebbe we can clean up enough in the creek so's she won't guess."

Ray was not listening. Transfixed, he stared at the rock wall opposite.

There, the shock of the coal fall had dislodged some sort of facing and exposed a portion of sheer black wall. Into the center of that small, gleaming patch thrust a great diamond-shaped head, wedge-mouthed, with star-ing, lidless eyes.

Down to Moars'

"Well, I'll be a spotted son of a gun!" Uncle Dream breathed at last. "If that don't beat all. Looks like a snake plastered against the wall, don't it?" He moved so that the light from his lamp swept along the wall, but beyond the pinched-in neck and a foot or two of thickening body, there was nothing to be seen. Perhaps it was just as well. If it *were* a snake, there was bound to be more of it than either Ray or his uncle cared to see.

They stared upward, fascinated, until at length Uncle Dream reached with his pick to give the ugly thing a prod. The pick-head chinked against stone.

53

"Hah, 't'ain't a snake atall," Uncle Dream exclaimed. "Just a freakish shape in the rock."

"I dunno." Ray was doubtful. "I read in some book they got snakes thirty-forty foot long in South America. Maybe they used to have 'em around here too, and this one's a fossil."

Uncle Dream tore his gaze from the staring head above. "Fossil? What's that?"

"Well, sort of a stone cast of an animal or whatever." He was not really sure. "It happens after they get killed or die. Just fills up around them. I think." He picked up the wagon handle, ready to go. The thing made him nervous, and his light was growing dimmer by the minute.

Uncle Dream was not to be hurried. He considered the thing on the wall as if it were a puzzle he was bound to solve. "Doesn't seem right such a thing ever could've lived in the Hollow or Up Top. Not forty foot long and with a mean look like that. It don't fit somehow. Not with redbud trees and bee-balm and starflowers. Come right down to it, I don't much like havin' it *under* Twillys' Green, neither—fossil or no."

As Ray watched, Uncle Dream—Uncle Dream of the soft voice and round-shouldered stoop—moved suddenly, hard-eyed and intent. Before Ray understood his intention, his arm arced upward like a steel spring suddenly released and the pick smashed against the rock. The diamond-shaped head fell with a reverberating thud and rolled away as Dream's arm swung up again.

"No!" Ray did not recognize his own voice, ragged with anger. "You'll ruin it! You'll ruin *every*thing."

Shards of the tapered neck lay on the dark floor. Ray dropped the wagon handle to grope frantically for the pieces, trying to fit them together. "Why'd you have to do that?" he raged wildly, senselessly, almost in tears. "It—it might've been valuable. We might've got a lot of money for a thing like that."

Uncle Dream was watching him in astonishment. Ray fell silent. Maybe he still could . . . but not now. Later. He could come back later. "What's got into you, boy?" Uncle Dream reached down to help him up. "It's only an old bit of stone. Who'd want to buy an old piece of stone?"

"Nobody," Ray said sullenly. "Nobody, I guess. I—I just don't like to see things broke," he finished lamely. He dusted off the knees of his jeans and turned to follow his uncle, who had taken up the wagon handle and moved down the dark corridor.

"Some things is better broke," came back the gentle answer.

In the outer cave they stowed the tools and lamps and shoveled the coal into buckets.

"You take them two down to your Aunt Star when we've had a wash." Uncle Dream indicated the smaller of the buckets. "And don't you let on about that little accident. We'll take us a little dip in the crick. You can flap your pants 'n shirt clean enough, but I'll have to rinch mine out and go along Up Top t' dry myself by Aunt Mavee's stove." He eyed Ray with concern. "You sure you're feelin' all right, boy? You sounded half-cracked in there for a minute."

"I'm all right." Ray evaded his eyes. In the half-light of the cave his panic already seemed foolish, baffling. He did not want to think about it. Hoisting the two buckets, he ducked through the low opening and stepped out into the day.

He felt better after the shock of the cold creek water. His arms had stopped trembling, though he still felt a little weak in the knees. He edged gingerly along the plank across the creek, teetering between the two buckets.

That mine. Fat chance he'd ever go in *there* again. But he had no sooner promised himself that than he began to wonder what the fossil might be worth. How much would it fetch from, say, a museum, like the one they talked about having in Apple Lock? Say in Huntington, or Charleston? There must be museums in big towns like that. Besides, Apple Lock would expect you to give it for free. So far, all they had in the way of rocks was a couple of fern fossils, half a horseshoe crab one, and a big boulder of brain coral: stuff that had come out of people's attics and garages during the Treasure Hunt they'd had to start the museum fund drive off.

Ray dawdled down the path past the deserted house at the head of the hollow to the Clewarek house. The snake now, that was different. Really rare. It might be worth twenty, twenty-five dollars. More than enough for the bus fare back north. The trouble was, most of the thing couldn't be got at—assuming that the head could be cemented together. Still, twenty-five dollars . . .

He would go to Charlene and Marv's. Old Charlene was the easiest to get around. He wasn't going to live with that Aura Lee, not even if his dad gave in about his staying. Not that he was likely to.

Rainelle was in the front yard when Ray reached the house, hunched up on the steps with a piece of paper and a pencil.

"What are you doing?"

"Nothing," Rainelle said. "Drawing."

Ray set the buckets down on the edge of the sagging porch and rubbed his chafed palms on his jeans.

"Who was that with you down in the rockhouse last night?" he asked abruptly. "And how come it looks so different out there this morning?"

"Huh?" said Rainelle absently. She kept on drawing, bent nearsightedly over the paper.

"Those folks," Ray prodded. "Whoever you were talking to in the rockhouse last night. And you—how come you were all got up in braids and those kooky clothes?"

Rainelle stared at him for a moment in complete bewilderment and then, just as a light seemed to dawn, her face grew blank, a window suddenly shuttered. Changing the subject, she sighed and said, "I seen Delly walkin' Sweet William down by the crick. He purely loves that baby. But he's got his misery look on. I bet you he asked Sue Ellen to marry him and she's said no again."

"So what?" said Ray, only half sidetracked. "He's kind of scrambled in the head, isn't he?"

"Only sometimes. And that wouldn't matter if she was sweet on him." Rainelle turned her unseeing gaze down the Hollow. After a moment's silence she said unexpectedly, "Delly, he seen them folks."

Ray did not understand.

"You know, the ones out in the rockhouse. The girl and the woman and man. Sometimes there's others. Mary-Mary's seen 'em too. You and Delly and Mary-Mary." Her tone was polite but firm. The implication seemed clear.

Ray sputtered. "I d-did see you! Or somebody like enough to be you. Don't you call me a liar."

Rainelle turned and looked at him in astonishment. "I didn't say you was. I said Delly and Mary-Mary seen them. Mary-Mary don't always understand what she sees, but Delly, he couldn't lie good enough to fool a doorknob. And he ain't *crazy*."

"How come they had him in the nut-bin up at that VA hospital then?" Merle had told him that. Something about a head injury.

Rainelle glared. "Anybody ever tell you you got a mean mouth?"

She looked like a bellicose fawn, timid and furious, and the incongruity made Ray grin. The anger that had swept him up ebbed away as suddenly as it had come. Rainelle was an odd one for sure. "Look," he said placatingly. "How could those folks live here and *no*body else ever see them? There's no way."

"I don't know." Rainelle was uncomfortable. "There's them woods Up Top. Where our grand-folks oncet lived."

Ray was doubtful. After all, he'd seen the girl—he found himself accepting that it had not been Rainelle— he had seen her down here in the Hollow. "Those old folks, the Dreegos, they'd know if somebody besides them lived up above, wouldn't they?"

"Might, might not," said Rainelle mysteriously. "Uncle Penn, he don't let on half what he knows about these hills, Daddy says. You know, I asked Aunt Mavee oncet if it was hants Mary-Mary seen. I thought maybe they was."

"Haunts? *Ghosts*, you mean?"

Rainelle nodded.

"What'd she say?"

"She allowed," Rainelle said uneasily, "as maybe they was and they wasn't. Something about how we're 'here and now' and mebbe they're 'here and then,' which is why we can't see 'em."

"What kind of riddle is that?" Ray asked in disgust.

Rainelle shrugged. "I couldn't make it out neither. Unless—unless it was kind of a roundabout way of sayin' Delly and Mary-Mary might be sort of disconnected from here and now."

"Well, *I'm* here and now," Ray grumbled. "She was pulling your leg. I bet you somebody up there's running a big old moonshine still, and they don't want anybody to know about it."

As a theory it presented difficulties. But true or not, the idea had possibilities. He thought for a moment and began to feel quite pleased with himself. "I better dump this coal," he muttered. "I'll see you later."

One bucket he emptied into the bin on the porch,

and the other in the battered coal scuttle next to the stove. Aunt Star, stirring up a batch of biscuits for lunch, smiled a little wearily.

"Thank you, Ray honey. You can put the buckets out on the back stoop if you've a mind to. No need to trot 'em back up right now."

When he had done so, Ray slipped up to the loft and hauled his duffle bag out from under his bed. Opening it, he rummaged for the tablet of lined paper and the ball-point pen Aura Lee had given him, saying, "Now mind you write to me'n your daddy regular." Well, he wasn't going to write to Aura Lee, not now or ever. Charlene, now, she could be trusted to pass a letter around so it would get to his dad and Aura Lee just the same. Sitting cross-legged on the bed, he chewed on the pen for a moment and then began to write in his neatest hand.

Dear Charlie and Marv,

This is a great place. I didn't have to go to school today. The kids here are Raynell and June Ann and Mary and Jody. Raynell and June Ann only go to school some times and Mary and Jody don't go at all so I think Im going to like it a lot. I went down in a coal mine today. A piece of the roof fell in on Uncle Duram but he wasn't hurt really. Uncle Duram and Aunt Star are nice. They don't ever yell. Theres this neat guy here with real long hair and a leather shirt fancier than Mo Fishers. I think he's got a still up by Uncle Pens. Yesterday

I tasted some white lightning and man! Its something. Tomorrow Im going up To visit uncle Pen
and Aunt Mavy Drego. They are real old and say
there are maybe ghosts that live here.

Your brother,
Ray

The bit about the moonshine would make Susie wild.
Charlene wasn't teetotal, but Susie was, and she'd start
fussing as soon as she read that. On second thought he
crossed out the ghosts line. That was laying it on a bit
thick. After recopying the letter, he looked for one of
the stamped addressed envelopes Aura Lee had put in.
Crossing out the *Mr. and Mrs. Perry Siler* and the
R.D.1 address, he wrote in *Mr. and Mrs. Marvin Siler*,
431R Front Street, Apple Lock, W.Va., stuck the letter
in, and sealed it up.

It just might work.

There was no mailbox closer than Moars' Store, so
Ray had to wait until afternoon, when everybody was
going down. Today, the first Friday of the month, was
county welfare day, when all the hollows emptied down
into Moars' Corners to wait for Bill Maclehose and the
mail. From Rainbow Creek and the remnant from Sour
Creek, from Akers and Muddy Hollows, from Horse
Hollow and High Hoop and No Hoop, and Twillys'
Green, everybody came. UMWA disability and pension
checks and Social Security pulled some of the old folks
down on other days, but first Fridays each month were

a lot noisier and more sociable, Aunt Star said, because that's when all the folks with kids were down—more than ever this year when there just weren't jobs to be had.

The Twillys' Greeners gathered across the creek below Yantos', with the little kids clambering all over Roney Yanto's old truck. Merle circled the truck, kicking the tires with a serious, critical air.

"Looks O.K. to me," he observed knowingly. "That old left rear blew out again last week, though. Inner tube's got more patches than a quilt. Pa says next time he oughta pump it full of cement 'stead of air. Couldn't do worse than now."

"Pretty good truck, though," observed Uncle Dream from where he leaned, propped against the tailgate with his hands deep in his overall pockets. "I remember when your daddy bought it, back before the coal bust. He was doin' pretty good back then. Got it paid off just before he was laid off. You sure won't find them fancy new Fords lasting any twenty-eight years."

Uncle Harry Mattick smiled. "Not so many trucks got two such good mechanics. I bet you and your dad ain't got two original parts left in that old rattle-bang."

"Well, maybe two." Merle grinned.

Cousin Roney was last to show up. Everyone was there but Uncle Penn and Aunt Mavee, who rarely went down to Moars', so when Roney came, the men and boys headed on down the road in a straggling group. Ray wondered why they didn't pile all the rest into the truck, but when the first knot of walkers had reached the bottom of the first long, steep grade, he found out why.

"Here she comes!" Adney Tullo yelled.

Everybody dove for the side of the road. With a dreadful coughing and clatter, the old pickup bounced down from the crest, rolling fast, bucking from rock to rock. As it flashed past, Ray had a glimpse of Cousin Roney clutching the wheel in rigid concentration, while Merle hung out the window on his side and yelled, "Geronimo-o!" The dog Patches bounced around in the back end, barking himself sick with delight and terror.

Erla, Luce, and Star came a-ways behind, with Opal and Sue Ellen. Cousin Faye and the girls came after. Jody and Sweet William, too little to walk much of the way themselves, were passed from uncle to aunt to cousin and back again. Down by the Rainbow Creek cutoff they were set on their own two feet for the last quarter mile.

"Why didn't they stop the truck back when we got to the easy grade and give everybody a ride in?" Ray asked. "You don't need such good brakes along here."

Delly, beside him, gave a rare, slow smile. "They'd never get it started again. Once it's stopped, it dies and kind of likes to rest a half hour or so. Roney brings it down mostly so we don't have to tote the groceries up ourselves. Used to be Adney and his dad had an old mule and a wagon, and we'd haul the groceries up in that and ride the womenfolk and babies up in the truck; but the mule died four-five years ago." Delly's thin face had a pensive look. "I always liked that mule."

The Corners was as busy as Apple Lock on a Saturday afternoon. A yellow school bus had pulled up beside the store and was disgorging a noisy stream of children. Along the store's front porch men sat swinging their legs, chatting, and spitting around chaws of tobacco. Bill Maclehose and the mail had not arrived yet. Every once in a while one or another of the men would rise, walk down the dirt road a few yards, and come back shaking his head.

One old man gave a derisive yip. "Well, if it ain't Twillys' Green marchin' in like a parade! Who's your new drum major there, Ad?"

Ray was embarrassed to find that he was a good five or six yards ahead of the others, who had slowed when they saw that Maclehose was late. He dropped back beside Adney and Dream but still felt every eye on him as he posted his letter in the bright red and blue box at the corner of the porch. To his dismay he had to stand around and nod politely as he was introduced to Boddies and Frews, Cassies and Gollens from Muddy, High Hoop, and Horse.

Uncle Dream and Adney fell into conversation with a Mr. Smale from Moon Hollow, over the ridge from Horse; something dull about the old mine there being closed out and augurs being brought in to work the south ridge, a spur too narrow for deep mining. "They already made a cut along the ridge an' just shoved that over-burden down off the edge," Smale complained. "Next good rain we get, it's gonter slide right down my corn-field. When everybody else left, I thought I could stick it out. Now it looks like 'git out or git plowed under'."

Ray took his chance and slipped away.

Inside the store a group of girls, ten or twelve of them, were perched on the brightly-patterned hundred-pound sacks of cow feed stacked along the front wall, giggling and drinking red pop or orange crush. Getting past them was like running a gauntlet. Pointedly ignoring the whispers and giggles, Ray headed for the battered red cooler, which he had missed the day before.

Finding a Dr. Pepper, he wandered down the far left aisle, where bolts of oilcloth hung on a wooden rack, and galvanized buckets and pans and water dippers lined the shelves above stacked washtubs and ashtubs. There were socks, bandannas, brooms and mops—even old-fashioned washboards, wood-framed with a ridged metal washing surface. A set of double washtubs mounted on legs was fitted with a hand wringer. He wouldn't have known what sort of contraption it was if there hadn't been a sticker on the rollers that said *WONDER-Wringer with Teflon-Coated Rollers Protects Your Fine Washables*. Hadn't they ever heard of clothes dryers? But for the Teflon and a stack of long cardboard boxes stencilled *Fidelity-King Television Aerial—Simple Installation, Simply Great Reception*, he might have been standing in the middle of 1935 instead of 1975.

The aisle along the rear wall was crowded with women with shopping carts, each with a smeary child or two pulling at her skirts and whining for pop or "lick-rish." The mothers ignored it all, chatting back and forth across other conversations. The women from Twillys' Green, Ray noticed, kept apart. Jody and Sweet William rode in their mothers' carts. June Ann followed Mary-Mary, who ambled along, taking things from one shelf and putting them on another. June Ann doggedly put each back where it belonged.

Up front, a cheer and a burst of laughter announced the mailman's arrival. Ray took a package of corn chips from the rack and headed for the checkout counters. There were already lines at both cash registers, and everyone in line seemed to have a full cart. With the check-cashing it promised to take forever, and Ray wished he had picked up a magazine or comic to read. He surveyed the candy bars idly and then scanned the shelves above: snuffs and chewing tobaccos—*Apple, Day's Work, Bull of the Woods*. More hick stuff, he thought impatiently.

As the line inched ahead, Ray found himself beside a crowded bulletin board. There were the usual wanted-to-swap signs: *Cordwood or oak shingles to swap for beagle or part-beagle pup*. A square card advertised *Races— Every Saturday Night—Willocks Speedway—Stocks, Stunts, You Name It*. A mimeographed sheet announced a rummage sale to benefit the Willocks Union High School band so that "our fine marching band can do us proud at the State Band Festival in Huntington."

LADIES! Quilters Needed!
said a neatly hand-printed card. *"Shops in New York City pay us $75 and up for quilts. Yes, AND UP. Contact Emily Robbins, Willocks 5726.*

One notice, laboriously printed on a square of lined

paper, invited one and all to come hear the Reverend Tom Lee Cooper of WSX Radio in Barkley, Tennessee, *"a special guest of our old friend Reverend Maclehose, who we'll all be glad to see again Saturday evening May 4 up at Hoop Church. Be there by 7. We'll have . . .*

Ray did not finish that one. His eye was caught by a word at the edge of a notice hidden just beneath it. Lifting up the Hoop Church notice, he read:

Snakes   **25**   *Snakes*
cents apiece
for snakes!

50¢ for copperheads.

JOIN CHARLEY DIXON FOR THE YEARS FIRST SNAKE HUNT! WE'LL BE STARTING UP NO HOOP HOLLOW WAY AND WORKING TORD BACHOP KNOB. MEET 7 A.M. AT HOOP CHURCH.

The date at the bottom was the previous Saturday's. Ray shivered. Weird! Who would pay good money for snakes? Rattlers, maybe. Up home, in Berman's Deli he had once seen a can of rattlesnake meat. One dinky little can cost over two dollars.

Ray was still frowning over the notice when a heavy hand clapped him on the shoulder and Mr. Moar's hearty voice said, "You ever been on a snake hunt, boy? You sure missed you a one last week. Old Charley Dixon, he's the best serpenteer around. Comes up from MacDowell County down in Kentucky, couple times a year. You get that uncle of yours to bring you along one time."

Mr. Moar disappeared into his office, and as the line moved up again, Ray took a look through the open door. Except for the path from the door to the desk, the stockroom-office floor was stacked with crates and cartons, half unpacked. A big old rolltop desk was adrift in papers. Shelving and battered wooden filing cabinets lined the walls. Along the desk top and cabinets, chunks of coal and specimens of rock held down more papers. Above the desk hung a large colored map of Withers County. It was one of the old school kind, mounted on cloth and hung from a wooden roller.

A second map, bearing the legend *Withers County, Section 8*, hung on the end wall, opposite the front window. On it various areas were colored in black, green, or blue, and to the upper left of center a small black square was marked by a little red flag on a pin.

Mr. Moar drew a large account book from a desk drawer and, turning, saw Ray watching. The jovial smile switched on.

"Come along in! Missis Smale there'll keep your place in line, won't you, Missis Smale?" As Ray edged in reluctantly, he waved a hand at the map on the end wall and drew him along. "Know where you are? This here's Moars' Store." He stabbed a forefinger at the little red flag. "I got a fellow down at the county seat to wangle me a copy of the biggest darn map they had. Five inches to the mile. See, this here's the Different River, and there's the Greenbrier, snakin' down from Twillys' Green Hollow."

Ray peered at Twillys' Green in the lower middle.

There, as in the other hollows, names had been pencilled in—Yanto, Clewarek, all the cousins' names—but there, unlike the other hollows, the names and boundary and elevation lines were strewn with little question marks. Trailing vaguely out across the area Ray supposed was the Greeners' "Up Top" was the name Dreego. It looked considerably larger than he had expected.

"Not a soul around here I don't know where he lives," Mr. Moar boasted. "Arbie Moar, he knows everybody and everybody knows Arbie Moar. Well, now, come along, boy. I got to get out there with this book an' make sure that soft-hearted Missis Moar don't cash them checks without settlin' up the back accounts."

"How come Twillys' Green's the only place not colored in?" Ray asked, as he followed Mr. Moar out.

"Beats me." Mr. Moar shrugged and pulled the door shut. The Yale lock clicked. "That's the way it come. Say, how's the Dreegos these days? Must've been sad for 'em when Aunt Neva Tullo passed on last month. They'll be the last of the real old-timers now. We don't see 'em down here any more. They're keepin' well, I hope."

Aunt Neva Tullo was a new one on Ray, so he just made a vague noise of agreement on that. Then, since Mr. Moar seemed to be waiting for an answer, he offered, "They look O.K. to me."

"Glad to hear it." Mr. Moar nodded and began to work his way past the line. "Sorry, folks. 'Scuse me, Missis Boddie. I just need to get by here."

When Ray's turn at a cash register came—at last—Bonnie said, "Forty-two cents. Fifty-two with the dime you owe me."

Uncle Dream had given Ray his dad's money order, and he had to turn out his pockets to find it. It was in his jeans, folded twice, and when he dropped it on the counter, something came with it: a shard of stone etched with scales and polished so that it had the sheen of feathers.

"Say, that's pretty." Bonnie picked it up. "Where'd you get it?"

Mr. Moar turned like a man in a dream over her shoulder as Ray, flustered, said, "Oh, just off the ground somewheres." It was a sliver of that spooky fossil. Funny, he didn't remember picking the thing up at all. "It's just an old piece of stone," he said, reaching for it.

Arbie Moar was faster. He picked it up and turned it over, rubbing his thumb against the smooth scales. "Now that is a pretty little thing," he said shakily. "I really do like that. How'd you come by it, Ray?" There was a queer frightening numb intensity to the man—as if, Ray thought nonsensically, he had just stuck his finger into a live lamp socket.

Ray shrugged uncomfortably, pocketing the bills and change Bonnie handed him. "Just picked it up off the ground."

Mr. Moar turned the stone over and over in his palm. "Tell you what," he said, switching on the cheery-storekeeper smile. "How about I give you a dollar for it? Fair enough?"

Ray stared. A dollar? For a splinter of stone no bigger than his thumb? "Sure," he said. "Why not?"

Mr. Moar reached into Bonnie's cash register to pull out a dollar. "There you are, Ray boy. You just made yourself a deal."

Bonnie goggled as Mr. Moar pocketed the stone and moved away. "Hmph!" she sniffed, as if to say "Some people have all the luck." All she said aloud was, "O.K., Rainelle, what you got?"

Ray had not noticed Rainelle just behind him. Apparently several of the women had passed her ahead of them. She slipped a small packet of sour lemon drops onto the counter and dug into her pocket for the fifteen cents. As Bonnie rang it up she gave Ray a scornful look. What did she expect him to do? Buy candy for one cousin and they'd all want something.

Mr. Moar had come back, still beaming. "Bonnie? You asked Miss Rainelle here yet?"

Rainelle looked startled. "Asked me what?"

Bonnie was uncomfortable. "Mister and Missis Moar want you'n me to sing for that service over at Hoop Church tomorrow night."

Ducking her head, Rainelle whispered, "But it's *Saturday* night tomorrow."

"Sure it is, and a very special one," Mr. Moar said smoothly. "We got Reverend Cooper comin' up. The one preaches over WSX? Why, your Aunt Neva Tullo used to listen to him regular."

"I dunno. I guess I could ask Daddy," Rainelle mumbled. Then she was off to the front door behind Ray.

Once outside, she leaned back against the door and drew a deep breath. "Oh, I *wish* we could go!"

"They pay you for singing?" Ray asked.

Rainelle was shocked. "In *church?*"

Ray shrugged. "You don't have to bite my head off. I was just asking. Anyhow, what'd you mean about it being Saturday night? Is there something special about Saturday night?"

The excitement in Rainelle's eyes died down. For a few moments they had lost their dullness and had almost a silvery sparkle. "I dunno," she said unhappily, and then softly, so that he had to strain to hear, she added, "It's just things—bad things just *happen* on Saturday nights."

She would not say anything more.

Encounter

Bonnie worked on her dad all through Friday supper.

"We *got* to go, Daddy. We're *good*. You know we're good. That preacher, he's bound to tell folks so down at his radio station, and I just know they'd invite us down. I bet WSM in Nashville's got people listenin' to all those little radio stations. I mean, you don't have to be in Nashville to get discovered."

There was a depth to Bonnie's nervous eagerness—a shadow in her eyes—that neither Roney nor Faye could fathom. Something had been eating at the girl for months.

"I wisht I understood how come you're so wild to get away," Roney said heavily. "Before long there won't be enough of us left to matter. Wilk and Verda Lillico gettin' kilt in that bus crash, Brother Hughie's family takin' off for Detroit after Ma died . . . now young Merle here's all the time talkin' about basketball scholarships and goin' off to Cincinnati. Won't be anybody left but old folks and cripples."

Bonnie paled. "Don't you call Delly no c-cripple," she flared. "Everybody talks all the time about how great Frank was. Well, Delly, he's . . ."

And then her sharp little face had closed.

"Right now you get out and wash that paint off before you eat another bite," Roney growled. But when she came back to the table, he said, "I'll talk to Dream. We'll see."

Uncle Dream hemmed and hawed, but finally consented—with the condition that Ray, Merle, and Delly, and some of the older cousins should go along.

Ray heard the news at breakfast and wondered what all the fuss was about. Up home, Aura Lee had practically dragged him off to church by the ear, and his own ma had never missed Sunday school, service, or prayer meeting. Yet here her kin were, fussbudgeting around because two girls *wanted* to go to church. Surely there couldn't be anything to all that "Saturday night" stuff. *So* Aunt Neva Tullo had a heart attack on Adney's back porch one Saturday night and all the dogs in the Hollow howled for a good hour afterward. The tale about a hefty bull calf being dragged off across the creek and devoured among the willows was spookier—the dogs had whined and cringed and refused to track the "varmint." Because there were no tracks to follow, the men could do nothing without the dogs.

There were other stories, but when Uncle Dream finished one off by saying heavily that at such times "the Hollow gits as dark as the insides of Jonah's whale and smells like mortality," Ray had almost sniggered out loud. As if weasels had never killed Aunt Mavee's chickens on other nights of the week or chill winds never sprung up after a balmy evening. Saturday coincidences blown out of shape by a bunch of superstitious hicks!

Still, they *were* going. . . .

Before his oatmeal was half-finished, Ray decided that if one sliver of stone were worth a dollar, a bigger one might be worth two. If he took another piece along to Mr. Moar tonight and let out casually that it seemed to be part of some animal, something really big, he might get the storekeeper interested enough to pay him for bringing it all out.

Slipping off to the mine unseen was something of a problem with Uncle Dream on his front-porch perch. Rainelle disappeared soon after breakfast, and the little ones crossed the creek to play with Erla and Cloyce's grandchildren. June Ann and her sniffles stayed inside. Ray hung around the front yard throwing sticks for Flower, the spotted dog, to fetch. The delighted Flower even found and brought back the one that landed on the outhouse roof, clambering up the stack of firewood that leaned against one wall. Uncle Dream sat with his cap down over his eyes and snoozed in the morning sun.

He seemed set for the day. Ray had given up and was about to go down to see if Merle was doing anything when his uncle tipped forward, pushed his cap back, and yawned.

"Think I'll go down to Yantos', see if I can give Roney a hand with the pickup. It was coughin' pretty bad yesterday. Like to come along?"

"I guess not. I don't much care about engines. Maybe I'll look around up here. Is it all right to go up that way?" Ray jerked his head toward the path that led up to Dreegos'.

Uncle Dream grinned. "Sure thing. Aunt Mavee, she's got the best strawberry jam you're ever like to taste. Bakes real good bread, too. When I was your age, I pretty near lived on her doorstep."

Ray, once his uncle was out of sight, dropped the stick he held and turned on his heel. Flower, abandoned, sat down in the dusty yard and whined.

The morning sparkled bright and warm in the tall grass and cool in the speckled shade of the scrubby willows by the creek. Yet the willows and the celandine, the wild sweet william and cuckoo-flowers might have been dust and rubble for all that Ray saw of them. As he passed the deserted house and stepped along the springy plank across the creek, he was calculating how much the snake would come to at a dollar a piece. Several of the chunks had been quite large, and there was more if it could be got at. Maybe he should charge by the foot. At thirty feet that would be thirty dollars.

Ray's eagerness shriveled a little when he came to the cave entrance. He hadn't recalled its being so small. Uncle Dream must have bent nearly double to get in. The gloom inside was somehow gloomier, too, but that he put down to imagination and his being alone. His mouth tightened as he remembered yesterday morning. Leave superstition to the others. He wasn't going to lose his head again.

Still, he was uneasy. He supposed there wasn't any danger of getting lost, not if he kept to the right, close to the rock wall. He set to gathering the things he needed. It took several tries with the spark-maker he had sneaked from a shelf in the cabin before he found a lamp that would light. Then he found two old gunny sacks in a dusty corner and loaded them and a pickaxe into the wagon. On second thought he went back to where he had found the gunny sacks and brought out a coil of rusty baling wire. No sense taking chances.

Beside the opening that led downward to the coal seam, Ray found a small, iron ring driven into the rock. Slipping one end of the wire through it, he twisted it tight and then started down with the wagon. It was awkward going, handling the wagon and turning the coil of wire so that it paid out straight, without kinks. It was so brittle with rust that it would take very little to make it snap.

Only at the bottom of the slope, alone in his dim island in the darkness did he feel the temptation to turn tail and run. For a moment yesterday's chill panic washed through him, but then it ebbed and was gone. Thirty dollars was a lot of money. And the air was warmer than he had remembered—quite comfortable, really. The air was sweet, without the acrid tang of coal dust that had been so heavy after Uncle Dream's mishap. There was supposed to be some sort of natural ventilation that meant the Hole was never plagued with dangerous pockets of methane gas. Wherever the draught came from, it was warm and scented, as if it blew off a sunny meadow. Strange that he hadn't noticed that yesterday.

One, two . . . four broad pillars on the left, and then you had to move out from the rock wall on the right because there was a ditch or something, filled with loose stones and rubble. That much he remembered. Only after he found himself in a timbered mine gallery with coal on both sides and retraced his steps, did he discover that he had gone straight ahead whereas the rock wall curved off to the right. Impatient with the wire—he would not have blundered had he not been so occupied with unwinding it—he let it drop and hurried on without it, all caution forgotten. He went along briskly, feeling increasingly pleased with himself until, stumbling over a rock, he stooped and found what he was looking for.

It was the serpent's head—in one piece except for an eye and a portion of bony brow that had been sheared off. The missing eye turned up at the edge of a pile of lump coal near the pillar opposite. Loading these and the rest of the shattered pieces was a matter of only a few moments' work. Getting any more of it off the wall was another matter.

The black rock of the wall—it looked something like obsidian or basalt, a volcanic glass—was covered over a great part of its area with a lighter, conglomerate sort of stone, almost as if it had been plastered over. It was the rest of this sheathing that had to come off. Ray swung the pick at a point just beyond the shattered neck and missed entirely. On the second swing he touched the stone, chipping off a piece and exposing a little more than a foot of the serpent's thickening body. And then he missed again.

What he needed were longer arms. Or to be a foot taller. The difficulty lay in the rubble-filled ditch, which prevented him getting a secure foothold closer to the wall. With planks or something like an old door to lay across it, he might manage. And there had been, he thought, a lot of short lengths of timber among the refuse in the cave.

On the way out, he took the wagon and the fragments he had already collected. More room that way for a fuller load next trip. When he came to the abandoned coil of wire, he retrieved it too, looping it up as he went so that there would be no chance of its getting snarled in the wagon's wheels. Ray felt relaxed, expansive, more confident than he had felt in a long time. With the money that was left over from the bus ticket, he might just buy a whole sackful of lemon drops for those poor, pasty little cousins who were stuck in this forsaken place.

And a box of chocolates to take along to Charlene. Soft-headed Charlene.

The air in the mine had grown warmer. The darkness was . . . *friendly,* almost caressing. Not in the least alarming. It occurred to Ray that this was somewhat peculiar, but it didn't seem particularly important, and the job of getting the wagon up the slope into the cave put it out of his mind.

He had to turn and haul at the handle with both hands. It was hard work, and once he had dragged the wagon clear of the passage, he leaned against the wall to catch his breath. He had to shut his eyes against the brilliant glare of daylight that shone in at the low cave entrance. When he opened them again, the light was gone, blocked by the tall shape of a man.

"Who—who's that?" Ray managed.

The answering voice was strange to him, strained and intent. "Ruan! *What have you done?* You bring ruin to us all!" That, at least, was what Ray understood him to say. How he understood it, he could not have said. The words themselves were strangely shaped and, though harshly spoken, oddly musical.

Ray's confidence melted like a June snowflake, and he was obscurely aware of some danger he did not understand. "I—I was only going to sell a bit of it," he faltered. "Uncle Dream, he doesn't want it. Mr. Moar gave me a dollar for just a little piece of it, so I thought . . . look, who *are* you?" When there was no answer, his resentment rose. "It isn't your snake."

"You do not understand. It is not your freedom that you buy, but the downfall of Berinir Gair."

Whatever that was. Ray tried to bluster it out. "O.K., I should have asked. Look, I'll just dump it all here and I *will* ask." Turning and tipping the wagon over, he tumbled the sackful of rock against the wall, muttering, "I don't even know who you are, spying after me. . . ."

As he turned, the man drew himself to his full height, stepping aside from the cave opening. Ray's voice failed. It was the man he and Mary-Mary had glimpsed at the window Thursday evening.

Long hair or no, there was an air of splendor to him. Of sadness, and of danger. *Perilous fair.* The words sprang to Ray's mind from nowhere; remembered, perhaps, from some long-ago book. He backed away, and in the moment he moved, the man was gone.

Just gone. As if he had vanished.

Ray, still clutching a piece of stone he had retrieved from the pile, shut off his lamp, threw it aside, and bolted out into the sunshine.

Hoop Church

"Now, that's real thoughtful of you, boy." Mr. Moar opened the crumpled paper sack and winked. "Think you'll make another dollar, eh?" And then he stared down into the sack, transfixed. The serpent's eye stared back, unblinking. Mr. Moar closed the sack hastily.

"Lordy, boy, what is it?" he croaked. He opened the sack again to peer in, caught like a bird by that unwinking stare.

Ray glanced uneasily around the dusty yard of the shabby little clapboard church. A handful of people stood by the steps, chatting with the frail old man who was Mrs. Moar's father, Brother Harkis, and another man, tall, neatly dressed, with a kind, lined face. The Twillys' Green folk were, as usual, off to themselves under a maple tree at the edge of the dusty parking lot —except for Sue Ellen, who was talking to Preacher Maclehose's son over by the graveyard wall.

Turning his back on the maple tree, Ray said casually, "It's off this big old petrified snake. I could maybe get you another couple pieces if—"

"A snake? What sort of snake?" Arbie Moar rolled the sack up and clutched it tightly. "Where'd you say this was?"

"Oh, just somewheres." Ray retreated into the sullen silence that he used on teachers and vice-principals when he didn't feel sure of his ground.

"Sorry, boy." Mr. Moar wiped sweat from his face with a big white pocket handkerchief. "None of my business, eh?" The handkerchief seemed also to have wiped the glitter from his eyes, for his face was round and jovial again. "It sure beats anything I ever saw. A real curiosity. Well, you turn up anything more, mind you give me first look at it." He pressed a bill into Ray's hand and turned toward the gathering at the steps.

Ray snuck a look down at his hand before stuffing the bill in his pocket. It was five dollars. Stricken, Ray darted a look across at Uncle Dream, who was still talking with Roney and Adney.

Five dollars!

Why, he might end up getting fifty, even more. The alarming encounter in the cave was quite forgotten. But the difficulties remained. He didn't see how he could get the whole thing out without letting someone else in on it. He was leery of that. Uncle Dream, he'd just *give* the thing away. Or want to divvy the money up with everyone in the Hollow.

And Arbie Moar was out. Outsiders couldn't get into the Hollow, to hear Merle tell it. Besides, Ray had a feeling that he couldn't trust Arbie Moar any further than you could throw an elephant.

The service, except for the music and the habit some of the older folks had of punctuating the sermon with *That's right!* and *Amen!*, wasn't all that different from services at Aura Lee's church up home in Apple Lock. But the Apple Lock First Baptist choir could never have made "Amazing Grace" soar like Bonnie and Rainelle did.

After "Amazing Grace" the girls sang something called "The Great Speckled Bird" that very quickly had Ray laughing behind his hand—until he saw the rapt faces in the congregation, and here and there a tear sliding down a wrinkled cheek. If the Great Speckled Bird stood for the Almighty, as it appeared to, Ray figured he must still be missing something, for it seemed to him vastly entertaining.

After the song Brother Harkis stood up to say how thankful they all were to have not just one minister offer to come for a visit, but two. "Preacher Maclehose is back with us tonight, and I'd like to ask him to step up here and take over, like old times."

Large, rumpled, and sleepy-looking, Reverend Maclehose looked around the crowded little church and observed drily that if they'd had this good a turn-out on
Sundays when Hoop was still on his circuit, Hoop would
still have a preacher. But then he reckoned a lot of folks
were here tonight just to hear his good friend Reverend
Cooper. He only hoped that being here might infect
some of them with the churchgoing urge.

At that, looking a bit less sleepy, he said they ought
to keep a sharp eye out for the dangers that beset a flock
without a shepherd. He bent a stern eye on the deacons,
sitting in a solemn row on the front bench, and boomed
out, "Like Saint Paul says in tonight's Scripture reading,
*Take heed therefore unto yourselves, and to all the flock
over which the Holy Ghost hath made you overseers—*"

He raised a warning hand, quoting without looking
at the Book. *"For I know this, that after my departing
shall grievous wolves enter in among you, not sparing the
flock. Also, of your own selves shall men arise, speak-
ing perverse things, to draw away disciples after them.
Therefore watch and remember."*

Drawing himself up impressively Reverend Maclehose
said, with a trace of irony, "Saint Paul went on to say,
*I have coveted no man's silver or gold or apparel. Yea,
ye yourselves know that these hands"*—he held up his
own large and callused pair—*"that these hands have
ministered unto my necessities and to them that were
with me. I have showed you all things, how that so la-
boring ye ought to support the weak and remember the
words of the Lord Jesus, how he said that it is more*

blessed to give than to receive. And when he had thus spoken, he kneeled down and prayed with them all."

During the prayer that followed, Ray snuck a look around and saw that a good half of the congregation was doing the same. Here and there he saw a few outright grins and some indignant glares, not to mention a general nudging and shifting in seats.

It was all over Ray's head. What had been so funny? Or upsetting? Arbie Moar had gone so purple in the face that he was loosening his tie, and Jessie sat beside him, eyes shut, rigid with either disapproval or apprehension. Ray could feel Cousin Adney's arm quivering as if he were laughing fit to kill, but his face was a reverent, prayerful blank.

Reverend Cooper, the radio preacher, was pretty good. He spoke on the text from Psalm 58, *Do ye indeed speak righteousness, O congregation? Do ye judge uprightly, O ye sons of men?* For all his being so thin and spindly-looking, there was a great deal of fire and thunder to Reverend Cooper. He came down particularly hard on hypocrites who were "brim full of Jesus on Sunday, and kicked Him in the shins the other six days."

The tension in the crowded room gradually lessened. There was a bit about "You live Jesus' way seven days a week, and just let the Holy Spirit light where It may. It's goin' to anyhow. And sure as hell—and I mean that seriously, my friends—as sure as you go runnin' wild after the Holy Spirit, you are goin' to stumble into the pits and the snares set for the unwary."

That raised some frowns, and when Ray saw Uncle

Dream lean forward to tip a wink to Adney, he knew that he was still missing something. But for the most part it was just a good, rousing sermon, and the congregation swayed and *amen*ed, and then it was all over, with everyone singing "How Great Thou Art." They sang, in fact, with such gusto that Ray was for a while carried out of himself and his discontents. When the collection basket came around, he fished in his pocket for a dollar bill, to drop it in.

Adney stared, and down the row Merle looked as if his eyes were going to fall right out into the collection basket. The basket was halfway down the row of chairs before Ray saw that he had put the fiver in instead.

The service ended with Brother Harkis calling down a vague blessing and announcing that because so many had so far to go home there would be coffee and cookies now, and afterward "any that wants to stay on fer our reg'lar Saturday—er, prayer meetin' is welcome to join our fellowship." But he didn't sound very encouraging.

Out by Reverend Maclehose's car Reverend Cooper shook Bonnie's hand and then Rainelle's. "You young ladies ever get down Tennessee way, you be sure and let me and Mrs. Cooper know. You make a real 'joyful noise,' and we'd be proud to share you with our radio audience some Sunday."

Bonnie positively glowed. Rainelle ducked her head, but the way she hugged her guitar it was easy to see she was pleased.

"You make a pretty joyful noise there yourself,

Preacher," Uncle Harry Mattick said, shaking Reverend Cooper vigorously by the hand. "Wisht we had a good sermon from one of you two every week."

Adney nodded in agreement. "Been a big fallin'-off this past year," he said, loudly enough for the little group of Hoop Church regulars back on the church steps to hear.

"Hush up, Ad. To hear some tell it, we're the chief fallers-off," drawled Uncle Dream.

Reverend Maclehose looked at him sharply. "Has Twillys' Green given up church-going, Dream?"

Uncle Dream lounged against the car, hands in his pockets. "Six months ago for me. I don't hold with all this snake stuff, always testin' to see how much grace the Holy Spirit's laid on you. That was some pretty sharp hintin' around you did in there tonight, Reverend, but if it was me, I'd've said it right out."

Adney nodded vehemently. "Arbie Moar and his daddy-in-law are killin' this church. Mebbe we're a pretty lukewarm sort of Christian hereabouts—me more'n most—but I know it'd be a good thing if you was still preachin' up here reg'lar, like before."

Reverend Maclehose opened the door of the battered old Pontiac and slid behind the wheel. "Ad, you know I'd not've left off preaching on the circuit if there'd been any help for it. Some of my churches never did have much to spare me, and with the price of gasoline and feeding the five youngsters still at home, and these deacons here at Hoop whittling down the expense money every other week, I just couldn't make ends meet."

The preacher pulled his door shut and rolled down the window. "Anyhow, things are looking up now I've got the church down in town. Maybe once I've cleared off my debts, I can afford to get up once in a while. Sunday afternoons, maybe." He started the engine and waited for his son Bob to climb in back. "Good to see you all."

Roney gave the old Pontiac a slap, and it snorted down the road.

"I don't get it," Ray said, when the car had gone and the Twillys' Green folk were drifting toward the road in the wake of the red taillights. "What was that about snakes?" He tried to sound casual.

Uncle Dream gave a look around. Most of the cars were gone, and the Hoop Hollow people who had been gathered in the wash of light down the front steps had disappeared inside. He looked at Ray thoughtfully. "You know what a holiness church is, boy?"

Ray shrugged. "I dunno. Kind of like Holy Rollers? Dancing and prophesying and talking in weird languages?"

"Well, now," said Uncle Dream cautiously. "Mebbe sometimes the Holy Spirit just does work that way. But your holiness churches now, they go a bit further. It says somewheres in the Scriptures that when the Spirit's on a believer he can pick up serpents and drink poison and it ain't goin' to hurt him. So these holinessers up and do just that, to see whether the Spirit's on 'em or not. Now this here church," he went on drily. "Jessie

Moar's daddy owns the land it's on, and old Arbie, he puts more in the basket than anybody else, so they pretty much get their way."

Ray was incredulous. "You mean they do that back *there*?" That was what the great snake hunt had been for then. The combination of Arbie Moar and snakes began to make him distinctly uneasy. *And* it didn't help to think that the five dollars Arbie took from one pocket might have floated right out of the collection basket into the other.

"Who knows *what* they do?" Roney said shortly. "It can't be good when Dessie Putz gets bit and says her husband and his old man *made* her handle one of them things at a service. That part don't sound like a holiness church. Holiness folks, they think different, but I never knew a one wasn't good-hearted. That church up t'other side of Bachop Knob, that's holiness. No, this here's somethin' else."

Bonnie clutched the collar of her thin little coat around her neck. "Brr-r! Makes me cold just to think on it."

"You?" said Merle with feigned astonishment. "Why, the box they keep 'em in was right under that chair you was sittin' on."

Bonnie gave a shriek and clapped her hands over her ears. When she saw everybody laughing, she tossed her head and stalked off, flinging over her shoulder, "Well *I'm* goin' home. The rest of you can stay and get bit for all I care." Her dim lantern bobbed away in the darkness.

Delly, who had not said a word all evening, mumbled

something about not letting her go alone and hurried off after her, with Sue Ellen and Rainelle not far behind. Delly's father lit the second lantern, and he and Adney and Roney moved off too. It was late, going on ten o'clock, and there were four good miles to walk.

Ray turned to stare back at the two brightly lit windows in the little box of a church, two square yellow eyes in the night. Out into that night came the thin sound of singing.

"You want to go have a look-see?" said Uncle Dream mildly.

Ray watched a silhouetted figure rocking jerkily in one yellow eye. "I dunno," he said. "No."

The lantern had already winked out of sight down the road that wound beside No Hoop Creek, and there was no moon, but Ray had been warned to bring his flashlight if he had one, and so they had a light and did not need to catch the others up.

They had gone perhaps a hundred winding yards down toward the county road when the wind rose. The rustle of leaves became a sigh and then a shriek. As the trees around them bent and swayed, Ray heard a roaring in his ears and took a buffet that sent him staggering to his knees. Half-stunned, he managed to raise the light and saw, quite clearly, Uncle Dream turning, his mouth open as if to shout a warning.

And falling.

Falling, with a short, black arrow feathered in his chest . . .

And then it was all dark.

Tekla

It was cold. Ray woke to a low murmur of voices and the chill, feathery touch of snow on his face. For a long moment he lay rigid, trying to think what had happened, where he was, why it should be snowing. And then he remembered the wind and Uncle Dream falling.

He sat up groggily. It was still dark and snowing thinly. Thinly, and yet the ground was covered. How much time had passed? A light guttered a short way off. A lantern left untended?

As Ray's head cleared, so did the blur that danced before his eyes. It was not a lantern, but a small fire shielded by a rim of heaped stones. By its light he could make out the body sprawled on the creek bank. He stared in dazed unbelief. Why should anyone want to harm Uncle Dream?

The mutter of voices died. Ray knew that he was being watched, but he staggered to his feet and ran, slipping in the slick snow, toward the figure on the bank, still under its veil of snow.

It was not his uncle.

Unaccountably, it was not Dream Clewarek, but the tall, long-haired man who had confronted him in the mine-cave. He had been shot twice. The arrows were short stubby things, quilled with turkey feathers. Wild turkey, Ray thought irrelevantly. His dad had once shot a wild turkey for Thanksgiving. . . . And there his mind stuck.

"What's this, Ruan?" A harsh voice rasped beyond the fire. "A bit late for regrets. Come, leave the carrion, or we will leave you here to keep it company. The messenger from Highness Tekla says that they have found the climbing trail to this Tûl Isgrun without you, so you have not yet bought your life even though you lured this fellow to us. Come. With this well-chanced snow we can follow their tracks without you if you repent your bargain."

Ray rocked back on his heels, unsteady, staring numbly.

The speaker drew in his breath with a hiss and strode across to give Ray a sharp blow on the shoulder. "Come, runaway," he sneered. "It is too late to stick your tail between your legs and whine like a frightened puppy. Who knows? Perhaps you will escape your lady's punishment. But you have brought us all a great distance on the trail of an old tale, and if there is no truth after all to this legend of the Dark Shrine, you will have much to answer for."

Ray could only gape at him. The man was dressed in a dark tunic embroidered with strange bright signs. His legs were bare, but he wore a warm fur cloak of deerhide lined with some softer fur, dark and striped with white. His short boots were fastened with silver buttons. Most astonishing of all, the front two-thirds of his head was shaved, and the lock at the back was bound in a gleaming knot. On his pate sat a small flat cap garnished with two feathers, and owing either to his assurance or his ferocity, it did not look at all absurd.

"In order, there!" the man rasped at his companions. There were four of them, dressed in much the same fashion, but not so richly. Their tunics were a darkish olive with a yellow sign on the breast that looked like a cross between a heart and a turnip. Their heads were shaven so that only a shortish round tuft at the back remained.

Ray's mind had begun to move, but haltingly. If he were not in Withers County, West Virginia, where was he? And *when*? The outlandish getups, the strange speech that somehow he understood: he could make nothing of it. Clearly they had mistaken him for someone else—a runaway captive or servant, apparently. And where had he heard the name *Ruan* before? Fearfully,

Ray looked down at his own clothing, and his stomach churned sickeningly. For it too was strange: warm leg-wrappings, a blue tunic, and a soft rabbit-skin cloak.

The man—his men addressed him as Kon—was looking at Ray sharply. "Something stirs in that slave mind. Did you not know we would kill the Watcher? Would that be it, dog Ruan? Well, now, perhaps the little dog still has teeth." The sneering voice rose. "Here, you, Bikaa. Bind the lady's slave. We'll not risk him slipping away to raise an alarm."

Ray, far too dizzy and bewildered to have raised an alarm in any case, felt his arms wrenched behind his back and secured with a thin cord, and his mouth gagged with a sweaty rag that had been the man Bikaa's neck-cloth.

The captain, Kon, moved to unbuckle something from around the waist of the fallen man, and Ray saw with deepening panic that it was a sword—long, straight, heavy-hilted, and sheathed in a scabbard of leather set with silver. Kon stripped away the gold collar and a string of beads as well, and Ray saw with wonder in the firelight that they were pearls.

"Huh!" Kon snorted. "If these are your Watchers, they will need to be more wakeful than this one to stop the warriors of Kanhuán."

Ray's mind darkened and he stumbled as they drove him along the creek bank.

The men moved as silently as the snow itself, hurrying at a half-run down the track that followed close beside the dark water of the creek that should have been No Hoop. Huge white oaks hunched over the trail, wide-boled grandfathers of trees. The rising moon gave no light at all through their thick veils of new leaves, but the men went swiftly, single file, in the darkness. Ray was forced to keep pace.

He was turned completely around. Where was the Hoop Hollow road? If the world were not completely upside down, they ought to be coming to the county road before long. Yet how could these—these *warriors* belong in a world that had county roads? Only in a dreamed world . . .

They did not come to the county road. Short of where it should be, they stopped in a clearing that, but for the monstrous oaks and beeches crowding close around, might have been the clearing where the No Hoop and the Greenbrier joined. And there was no road leading down to the water, only the narrow track. The center of the clearing was trampled with the prints of many feet, blurred now, and filled with snow. The log bridge across the forks—a bridge that had boomed pleasantly with every footfall—was not there.

There were stepping-stones in the smaller stream, and it was that way that the little company turned, moving upward on the trail that hugged the higher stream. They had traveled perhaps three miles when stream and path turned sharply into a steep gully. The path, to keep its foothold, climbed sharply to the shoulder of the hill. Ray, stumbling with weariness and lack of sleep, felt a deepening dread. The trees were all wrong, but still it was terribly like Twillys' Green's hill. Suddenly he had a bone-deep feeling that it *was* the same hill and that, beyond all reason, the stream that tumbled below *was* the Greenbrier.

He had to be dreaming. *I'm in bed at Uncle Dream and Aunt Star's, and I'm dreaming.* He clung to the thought desperately. But the foul rag that bit into the corners of his mouth, and the cord that chafed his wrists were not the dull fearful aches of dreams, but a bitter, wakeful sharpness. And for all the strangeness of the great dark trees and the roadless hill, the shape of the land itself was inescapably familiar. The track and creek crested the hill together, crossing paths where a wooden footbridge spanned the spillway of a small pond: the same and not the same.

Some fifty yards along the tree-crowded gap, as in the approach to Twillys' Green Hollow, the hills drew back. But here there were no shack-dotted bottomlands, no barren hill-fields. Great trees marched up the sides of the rising moonlit valley. The stream sang down from the wooded highlands, pouring like dark music among the rocks, a nervous line inked down the middle of a narrow ribbon of meadow. Ray shivered uncontrollably at that still, nightmare beauty.

His captors had stopped in awe. One, a short man wearing a cloth helmet and two tunics against the cold, trembled and said, *"Ai, kowan'm teewah'a Goskorza!"*

"Solat!" snapped Kon. He pointed.

The tracks they followed led to the stream and up its winding course. The men went on, looking about them fearfully, as if at any moment enemies might spring upon them from under the eaves of the dark wood. But they gained mid-hollow without mishap. There the trees closed ranks across the stream, and still no attack had come.

"This way," whispered Kon. He gestured upward through the trees. They had not gone far into that darkness when, turning abruptly, he led them up to the right, away from the stream and toward a glimmer of fire.

The fire was in the rockhouse. The door stood half ajar, and inside firelight flickered. It flamed outside as well, where pits had been freshly dug to shield small fires. Shadowy groups of men took shelter around their warmth. Many men. Most were dressed, like Ray's captors, in blackish green, the same heart-turnip emblem on the tunics. Several wore feathered caps like Kon's. An older man in a rich beaver cloak wore an antlered headdress made from a deer's skull.

As Kon's men approached, the small knot of men around one fire parted, and Ray found himself face-to-face with the most alarmingly beautiful woman he had ever seen.

She was young, or seemed to be so. Her black hair hung in untidy waves below her waist, and her eyes gleamed yellow as cats' eyes in the firelight. Her richly-patterned skirt was short, and on her breast hung a long necklace of pearls and polished bears' teeth. Its round hoop-snake pendant was carved in jade. The cloak thrown back over one shoulder was of beaver with the nap sheared into curious designs and richly stitched with pearls. Her smile was frightening.

"Ah, my little slave-dog come cringing back! It was foolish to think you could slip the leash, Ruan. I must think what to do with you. I would have thought the whip gentled you long ago."

Kon bowed low. "Highness Tekla, we followed the runaway up the western valley and, losing our way, searched the whole of it for him and for the shrine you seek. We were on our way down again when we came upon this one being tracked by one of the Watchers your old tales tell of."

The woman drew in her breath. "Did he call himself such?"

"No, Wisdom. Had I stopped to ask, we five would be stretched out in the snow, and he should long since have raised a hue and cry against you. No, his sword speaks for him." So saying, Kon unbuckled the sword from his waist and handed it across the fire, hilt first.

Tekla seized it, her eyes gleaming. With her finger she traced out the silver figures on the scabbard. Then, grasping the hilt in one long-fingered hand, she drew the blade and whirled a flashing silver circle in the air. The men drew back in astonishment.

"It is some magic!" she whispered. Her eyes exulted in the shimmer of the long, slender blade. "Pakán!" she commanded abruptly, pointing at one of the men. "Stand here and offer me your sword against this."

The man she had indicated stepped forward nervously. Drawing a short, broad sword from under his cloak, he planted both feet as firmly as he could in the muddy snow and thrust out his blade. It gleamed with the dull red glow of copper.

"Aka kuutlá!" hissed the woman. Swinging the long blade with both hands, she slashed silver fire across the darkness.

There was a moan, and a great murmur. The men nearest him rushed to the man Pakán, who stood staring at his severed sword and a forearm gashed to the bone.

"That," said Tekla with a grim smile, "should be magic enough to explain what some of you have sneered at as our 'night-skulking.' I do not wish to meet these tall legends in open battle." She smiled contemptuously. "The boy says that there are few of them, but if any of those few are the remnant of the Ancient Ones, two or three together might serve to rout you all."

The old man in the beaver cloak looked disapproving. "Old wives' tales," he grumbled. "These folk bleed as well as we do. They may bear weapons worthy of gods, but that is no reason to think them more than men."

Tekla rounded on him in a fury. "If that is so, Hakán, they are better men than you, and these—these *krekarn*! When my father was alive, the *gath* was made of men, not creatures like these pygmies of my brother's. Because our father was a giant, and he is not, he cannot bear the old *gath* near him. But by Kuutlá, we could rule *twice* the ten cities of New Aztalán with the old *gath* and weapons like these!"

The old man held his ground, though his eyes were wary. "Is it weapons we have come for then?" he asked stolidly. "I could believe that Kanhuán might conquer the Ten Cities of New Aztalán had we all such blades, but I thought we came to find a darker, shorter road to power."

"Aye, so we have," said Tekla, shortly. "The Dark Shrine out of the old legends *is* here. I *know* it." Seeing the doubt in the faces around the low fires, she schooled her voice to softness and set about weaving a net of words to hold them to her will.

"Come, even Hakán has said that this place above all others is where the Lost Paradise of the Third Age must have been! And that is where the Dark Shrine of Power lies. You think it only a tale to frighten children? Old womens' superstition? That is because it has been hidden since before our people came from Old Aztalán, since the time of the coming of the Fishermen after the foundering of Umeár. I have traced it in rumor and dark tales from the rotting archives of Old Aztalán and the songs of the witch-women of Tuxclosan to shards of rock-writing in the dying fisher-villages of the eastern sea. At the root of the tales it is always the same."

Her voice fell away to a silken croon. "In the Third Age the Nameless Ones were bound beneath the mountains of Ebhélic and Hlannor, but after the foundering of Umeár one of the great ones broke free and tempted the fisherman Bedda. 'I know the secrets of darkness and all the treasures of the earth,' he said. 'They are yours if you will give me your shape to walk in now and again.'" Tekla smiled derisively "Now, Bedda was as greedy as any man, but he feared to be so close as that to such a one, so he sent his wife to the Aldar, who chained the Great One at the secret center of Ebhélic and set the Watchers over him."

Tekla's voice rose, shading from honey into venom. "But *I* am not so shy as Bedda. We are here because when this boy was captured by hunters and brought wounded to the temple in Kanhuán for sacrifice, I kept him instead for my slave. And why? *Because in his sick gibbering he spoke the name Túl Isgrun.* In the speech of Ebhélic that is 'The Dark Shrine.' It is that we seek: a shrine guarded by the sacred stone image of the One the witch-women call Katoá."

Turning, she said, "Come, ungag him." The men nearest Ray leaped to obey. As the rag was pulled away, Ray drew a long, shuddering breath.

"Quickly!" Tekla snapped. "How many of your kindred are left? Not the old women and babes. How many others?"

For a moment Ray could not swallow. "I-I don't know," he croaked. And then he cried out sharply as a hard hand squeezed the back of his neck. "I'm not sure," he gasped. "Fourteen or fifteen." It was the truth even if it was not the truth she sought.

"So many?" The woman's eyes darted uneasily to the open door of the rockhouse, then back to Ray. "Eleven at least unaccounted for," she hissed. "You dare to tell me so many? Under the whips you swore to six. No more. No, *solát*! Do not spin me yet another answer."

"Put him with the others," she ordered. "Until we have put a guard on every deer track and rabbit run we are in peril if there truly be so many. We are fifty, but we go on strange ground against strange enemies. When the guard is set, this slave will take us to Tûl Isgrun. Go, put him with the others."

Ray fell through the rockhouse door and through the bottom of his dream. If the wooded wilderness and the barbaric beauty of the savages outside could be dismissed as the phantoms of nightmare, the people in the rockhouse could not.

A woman and a girl lay on pallets by the fire. The woman, her head roughly bandaged, seemed asleep. The girl, disheveled, hawk's eyes glaring, vibrant, was more awake than any creature he had ever seen. It was the Rainelle-girl, but the difference between Rainelle and this one was the difference between the blind, velvety mole and the puma that hunted the long-ago hills. She was bound hand and foot, but she scrambled backward as if Ray had been a ghost.

"*Ruan*! It was *you* brought them here! But you are dead. Eloas said that the wolves of Tlegúro must have eaten you." Her voice hardened. "I see they did not, for it is these human wolves who have done so. They have killed Elathos. Did they tell you that?"

"Look," said Ray helplessly, raising to his knees. "I don't know what all this is about. I'm not this Ruan. I don't know what he's done. I'll untie you, if you want. Let me untie you."

She held as still as the deer before it bounds away, watching as he fumbled at the leather cords binding her wrists and ankles. Ray was clumsy, unnerved by her strangeness and the probing of those silver-pale eyes.

"Someone else was killed," she whispered suddenly, so that his fingers trembled on the last knot. "You were there. Was it my father? He has not come home from his hunting."

Ray was afraid to answer. How could she know?

"You are different," the girl said slowly. "They have eaten your heart out. It must have hurt. For that I am sorry."

"Please—" Ray said.

But she was scrambling backward away from him. Before he understood what she meant to do, she had snatched up a piece of firewood and swung at him—a glancing blow, but enough to send him sprawling into the fire. He rolled away with a yelp of pain, but by the time he had collected his wits, the girl had gone. Vanished. *Like her kinsman in the cave.*

But not quite. In the far dark corner, a bench had been dragged against the wall and the woven tapestry hanging there swayed, brushed by a pair of feet that wriggled upward and out of sight. A hole. There had to be a hole or fissure in the rock.

Ray hesitated barely a moment. The *gath* had ignored the crash and clatter. "Let the fools fight between themselves," they probably thought.

He climbed onto the bench and, reaching upward into the crevice, found the handholds cut there. He pulled himself up, and struggled for a knee-hold. The air inside smelled overpoweringly of smoke, and his hands kept slipping on the oily soot. He was almost too large for the passage, but inch by inch he moved upward, showered with the soot and dislodged stones of the girl's climbing above. The air was so thick with grime that he felt he could not breathe. When he did, he choked and his ears sang.

And then he could not move, and the darkness closed in around him.

A Bit of Research

Ray woke to a burning throat, a throbbing head, and ribs that ached with every breath he drew. It was several moments before he could bring himself to move, and when he did, he heard someone, a woman, say, "Oh, thank goodness!" He opened his eyes to find Aunt Star sitting beside the bed in her old hickory rocker from downstairs. The muslin sheet she had been mending slid to the floor.

"Dream!" she called. "Dream, honey?"

In a moment Uncle Dream's head poked up through the ladder well.

"He's woke up." Aunt Star turned her smile to Ray and took up his hand to squeeze it. "We feared your head was broke. Dream says you took a nasty fall."

Uncle Dream came across the creaking floor to lean over the bed, one hand on a low rafter. "How you feelin'? Roney and I was thinkin' we'd have to get that truck runnin' so's we could get you down to a doc in Willocks."

"My head hurts." The complaint came out in a weak croak.

"I should think so!" Aunt Star said. "It's a bad gash you got."

"Must've hit your head on a rock when you tripped," Uncle Dream said.

Ray gingerly reached a hand up to feel his head and found it swathed in bandage.

"I had to tie it pretty snug," Aunt Star said apologetically, "so's to hold the pad hard against the cut."

Ray felt hopelessly muddled. "What happened?"

Uncle Dream shrugged. "Reckon you tripped on a root or somethin'. This wind come up out of the blue— fiercest wind I ever felt. I turned around to grab aholt of you, and you were already fallin'."

It *had* all been a dream. Ray sank back in relief. The crack on the head had spun him into a nightmare so real, so strange, that he marveled his mind could ever have made it up. Didn't dreams have to come from bits and pieces already in your head? He felt too sick to puzzle that one out.

Aunt Star rose. "You sit here, Dream. I'll go down

and fix Ray a bite to eat. You'll eat a bit of supper, won't you, Ray honey?"

He squeezed his eyes tight to see if that would help. "Supper. What time is it?" They had eaten supper before they left for Hoop . . .

" 'Bout eight-thirty," said Uncle Dream. "That Sunday mystery movie's just startin' down on the TV. You can't hardly see a thing, but the girls is glued to it."

"I could make some toast," Aunt Star offered. "And boil up some soup. If you could get that down, and some herb tea, it'd do you good."

Ray promised to try. When she had disappeared down the ladder, he lay for a moment, thinking. He had been out far longer than the hours he had dreamed of. For one wild, crazy moment it came over him that he—no, Ruan—had been wedged unconscious in that rock chimney all these hours. But that was clearly nonsense.

"Uncle Dream?" he said hesitantly. "I had this dream . . ." He grinned weakly. "That sounds funny. How come nobody calls you Durham?"

His uncle smiled. "Your grandma always used to say I was a million miles away whenever there was chores to be done. I'd sit for an hour, watchin' some old wasp paper his nest, or a groundhog clearin' mud and leaf-trash out of his tunnel after a rain. I was always dreamin' what it would be like to be inside some other skin. Guess it just come natural for the family to bend 'Durham' into 'Dream'."

Inside some other skin . . .

Uncle Dream looked at him curiously. "What was you goin' to say about a dream?"

Ray told him—but only the bones of it, vaguely clothed. Not all of it. The fresh and vivid detail was still there, but he shied away from it, growing more and more uneasy. Unlike a dream, it had not faded. It did not play that quicksilver trick of dreams, sliding elusively away as they do in the telling.

"Well, now." Uncle Dream was troubled, the rocking chair still. "That is peculiar. My granddaddy, that's your great-granddaddy, he used to say there'd been folks in Twillys' Green forever. Lived Up Top, most all of 'em, except there was always one family down here, like in his day. This dream of yours might have some truth in it." He frowned. "There was this professor-fellow I talked to oncet down at Moars' wanted to come up here and 'study' us. Wouldn't believe we meant it when we said no. One thing he said was it looked like we'd maybe got some Cherokee in us. But, the Cherokees hereabouts was woodsy folk. I never heard tell of them havin' swords, like what you tell of.

" 'Course," he said, looking a little embarrassed, "there's them old fairy stories we was told when we was children. Mebbe if you just think back, you'll remember your mama's told you some of them stories when you was little. Come to think on it, there *was* folk called 'Watchers' in some of them yarns."

Ray struggled to sit up. The effort made his head hurt fiercely, but he was too interested to lie still. "*What* yarns? Mama never told me anything at *all* about Twillys' Green."

Uncle Dream shook his head. "I ain't heard 'em sincet I was six or seven. You could ask Uncle Penn, though.

He used to be a great old one for stories. You go ask Uncle Penn sometime."

By Monday morning Ray was making other plans. He awoke with a stiff neck, but the throbbing in his forehead had died to a dull ache. He dressed in the half-darkness. The sun rose earlier, but it was six before the hills let a little light in. When he heard Aunt Star moving about downstairs he went down and helped fix his breakfast of fried bread and syrup—not the pale watery stuff from Moars' but real maple syrup from the Dreegos' trees Up Top.

Afterward, on the pretext of going to the privy, he slipped out to the rockhouse and came back in a state of dazed excitement. The rock chimney was there. It was *there*. He had missed seeing it on Friday morning because it had been plugged up with a wad of old carpeting to keep the draught off one of the cots. Perhaps it had all been a dream, but at least part of it had been a *true* dream. What if it all had?

"You sure you ought to be out of bed, Ray honey?" Aunt Star left off pouring Uncle Dream's coffee in mid-cup. "You look kind of feverish to me."

"No, no, I'm fine."

He would not bother going Up Top. That could wait. Besides, what could the old man know? He must be over ninety if he was a day, and anybody that old had to be half-gaga. He needed facts, not old fairy tales. If such things as he had seen had ever really happened, if such people had existed, there had to be a way to prove it. And to tell the truth, he was already sorry he had told Uncle Dream. Why, he could not say.

At seven o'clock, with a reluctant Rainelle and June Ann in tow, Ray was off to the school bus. At the lower end of the Hollow, where the Greenbrier joined with a little spur stream and bent away toward the gap, they caught up with the Lillico children and then Merle. Dawn and Bob-White had been dawdling in hopes of missing the bus—and getting to poke around Moars' before adventuring back up through the woods with Delly, who always seemed to be around when the children were going up or down. Not that they really minded Ray chivvying them along. They did not particularly mislike school. But, as Bob-White panted when they scrambled aboard the bus, it was the "first time I seen anybody like to break his neck gettin' there."

Much of the morning at Bachop Area Junior High School was lost. It was a depressing place when you were used to the bustle and bright colors of Apple Lock: bare muddy grounds and dark, ill-lit corridors. Once Ray was registered, he sat twiddling his thumbs in the vice-principal's office while a schedule of classes was drawn up for him, and then in the nurse's office where, to his pain and disgust, the gash in his forehead was swabbed, stitched, and neatly band-aided. Then he sat and fidgeted through fifty minutes of a history class in which a woman teacher with a face as blank as a board read out of the textbook in a droning voice and

finished off by having the class recite in unison all of
the counties and county seats of West Virginia.

At noon Ray polished off his sack lunch as fast as he
could. On short notice Aunt Star had scraped together
bread and dripping sandwiches, dried apple rings, and
cornbread. It was dry going, washed down with half a
pint of milk from the cafeteria. Finished, he started looking for the library.

The library turned out to be located in one of the
"temporary" buildings, a weather-beaten structure that
must have been temporary since 1942. It was at least
cheerier than the rest of Bachop, for inside it had been
painted daisy yellow instead of the cat-sick color of the
rest of the school.

The librarian, caught in mid-sandwich, looked up
mistrustfully and complained, "They're not supposed
to send you people in here for detention during my
lunch hour."

"Detention?"

"Well, whatever. The library's closed." She gave him
an ironic look. "Unless you came for a book."

When Ray nodded, her eyebrows went up and she
said wryly, "I sure don't get many of *you.* Look, come
on in and shut the door. What is it you want?"

What he wanted did not seem to be there. There
was no history of Withers County, and the *Concise
History of West Virginia* was so concise that it took up
with the partition of Virginia and left off at 1902. Returning it to the desk, Ray asked, "Miss? You got anything about Indians from around here?"

The little librarian—the nameplate on her desk said

Miss Powe—reluctantly left her cake and coffee to show him to the oversize-book shelves below the back corner window. There, she dragged out a dusty volume, laid it on the window shelf, and went back to finish her lunch. It was an old book, *The Boys' Illustrated Book of Indians*. A *very* old book. From the faded, embossed cover depicting an Indian brave on horseback against the setting sun, Ray knew it wasn't going to be any help. The text read like gluey oatmeal, and the old engravings of portraits and scenery were equally stodgy. None of the pictured Cherokees looked particularly like either the Twillys' Green folk, despite the dark skins and high cheekbones, or Tekla's warriors, shorter and broad-faced.

Back at the front desk, Ray said, "I have study hall sixth period. Can I get a pass to come back?"

"You didn't find what you were looking for?" By now Miss Powe was eyeing him with mild interest. "What exactly is it?"

"Well," said Ray, "I want to find out what Indians lived around here. Who was here first, and all that, on up to the Cherokees. I guess they were toward the end."

"Oh." She seemed depressed again. "We wouldn't have anything about that. Most of these books are as old as the building, and the new-book budget is so small that by the time I order the books teachers request, there's hardly a dime left. Nobody's ever asked for early Indians. I suppose you could ask Mrs. Lunn. She teaches history."

Ray sighed. Mrs. Lunn wouldn't know anything that

wasn't in the textbook or on some list. The bell rang, and he moved to go.

"The only thing I know," Miss Powe said suddenly, behind him, "is that there used to be a really big Indian town up on the Kanawha River near Charleston, where I come from."

Charleston. Charleston wasn't all that far away. Ray tried to remember what the woman Tekla had called the place they came from. The Kanawha rang a bell. Kanahaw? No, Kanhuán! Ray's headache began to pound again, but he scarcely noticed it.

"This city, what's it like? What were the people like?"

"Goodness, I just don't know." She was a little startled by his eagerness. "It must have been a very long time ago, because there's not much left. No buildings. There were burial mounds, forty or fifty of them. They—" She broke off. "Look, you're going to be late to your class. Come back sixth period if you like, but there's really nothing here. I'll tell you what I will do, though. I can phone my brother up in Charleston tonight. There would be material in the library up there. He could have it xeroxed."

"I dunno." Ray was doubtful. "Couldn't he just borrow the library book?" Copying machines cost money, and at ten cents a page he couldn't afford much.

Miss Powe smiled. "I'll see what I can manage. But you'd better hurry now or you will be late."

The late bell shrilled as Ray ran down the main-building corridor, but since he was a new student the math teacher charitably assumed that he had had trouble locating the room and did not mark him on the tardy report. And Ray, to his own surprise, was in such good spirits, headache or no, that he scored an 85 on a surprise quiz at the end of the hour.

The school bus pulled into Moars' Corners at four o'clock. The younger children poured into the store, some to linger deliciously over spending their pennies and nickels, the rest to go shyly up and down the aisles deciding what they would have bought if they could. The older children sat on the porch in the sunshine or inside on the stacked feed sacks and joked and shared cokes. Merle had stayed for baseball practice, so Ray wandered about on his own for a bit and then bought two fat red licorice whips, one of which, after a great deal of pulling and twisting, he shared with Rainelle— but only when Bonnie had brought out a pair of scissors from under the counter and cut it for them. The other, snipped in three, Ray gave to June Ann and the Lillico children.

"How come you went to school?" Bonnie asked curiously, eyeing his bandaged lump. She grinned. "If it was me and I had a bed of pain, I'd lie on it."

Jessie Moar turned to look. "Mercy! That looks just *awful.*"

"Teach him to look where he's going," Bonnie said tartly.

"Why, it must hurt terrible," Jessie commiserated. "It's turnin' black and blue all down past your *eye*brow."

"Black eye? You got yourself a black eye, Ray boy?"

Arbie Moar came out of the office with a sheaf of invoices in one hand and a stump of cigar in the other.

"No, sir. I just fell and hit my head." Ray slid a dime across the counter for the candy and turned to join Rainelle.

"Whoa there, boy. What's your hurry?" Arbie beckoned jovially. "Come along back in here. Got something I want to show you."

Ray followed him into the office reluctantly.

"Here now, what d'you think of *that?*" From the desk drawer he brought out five crisp new ten-dollar bills and spread them out in a fan on the stained blotter. "There! You got me so all-fired interested in that fossil of yours that it's worth fifty dollars to me to see the rest of it."

Ray swallowed. "Well, there's a couple-three more pieces, but they're kind of an awkward size. Sort of heavy to get down here."

Mr. Moar held up a hand. "No, no. No need for you to hump it down here. When I said I'd give fifty just to *see* it, I meant exactly that." Noting Ray's suspicious look, he went on smoothly. "I figured, when I really thought on it, that the thing might not exactly be yours to sell, Ray. But if I see it, and it's what I think it is, I may just do some dickering with your uncle. Him and Star could use a little extra cash with a baby coming and all." Arbie Moar darted him a sideways look. "I guess it's in some kind of cave or old pot-mine, eh? It *is* on your uncle's land, I take it?"

"I—I don't know," Ray said. And he didn't. Moreover, he was surprised to realize that, even with the fifty dollars spread out on Arbie's desk, he might not have told if he *had* known.

Mr. Moar seemed to sense that he had been too eager. He dropped his voice and said with a confiding air, "The reason it's worth so much to me is that it's not going to be easy to *get* to see it. Uncle Penn Dreego, he's a fine old man, but he keeps to the old Twillys' Green ways and that old mistrust of 'furriners,' and blamed if all your kin don't go along with him. Only fellow I ever knew t'get in there was the school truant officer once. *But*"—he gave Ray a wink—"but if I was to slip up some evening . . ." He let the words trail off suggestively.

"Look, I—we got to go. I'll think about it," Ray mumbled uncomfortably, edging out of the office. Once out, he hurried toward the door, snagging Rainelle as he passed the checkout counters.

"Hey, there! Wait a minute," Bonnie shrilled, waving a long, white envelope after them. "I almost forgot. This is for Cousin Dream."

Rainelle went back for it, and then they slammed out through the swinging doors.

Arbie Moar's words had stuck in Ray's mind. Uncle Penn again. Maybe he *would* go see Uncle Penn.

Up Top

The Dreego house was huddled out of sight behind the great rock outcrop at the head of the path up from the Hollow, a low stone building shadowed by great beech and hemlock trees. A series of stone walls and low-roofed outbuildings made it look vastly larger than any of the houses below.

Ray and Uncle Penn sat on a stone bench in the middle of Aunt Mavee's herb garden with a plate heaped with buttermilk cookies between them. "It was only a dream," Ray finished lamely, "but I thought after I saw the rock chimney that maybe some of the rest of it was true too." As with his uncle, he had left out the bit about Tekla's search for something called Tûl Isgrun. He would have liked to ask about the mine-cave and the fossil too, for if Uncle Penn didn't think them anything special, then he did not see that there would be any real harm in sneaking old Arbie Moar in for a look. He did not ask because, harm or no, he didn't want it to be all right. Arbie Moar gave him the creeps.

Old Uncle Penn shook his head wonderingly and drew on his pipe. "I never did hear such a tale! When I was a boy, I thought oncet I seen a feller dressed in skins, but it was a foggy morning and I didn't see him clear. Never saw him again, neither."

"You think it was just a dream? That none of it ever did really happen?"

"Whoa back! I never said that." The old man cleared his throat and spat. "You say they called the folk here 'Watchers.' Well, that's wrong to start with: the way I heard it there never was but one Watcher. Most've forgot it now, but in my youth the old folks used to say they'd always been a Watcher here in the Green. My granddaddy he was one, though he didn't call hisself that. And his daddy was before him. Goes back quite a ways. 'Back to the third,' folks used to say. I never did know what that meant. Prob'ly just a manner of sayin' 'way back when'." He rubbed a gnarled hand across a bristly white stubble of beard. "Reckon that means *I'm* it now."

Ray doubted that, but he held his tongue. Surely if

you were set to watch something—or for something—
you would know what it was. Ray had left that part
of the story out, but the old man hadn't even noticed the
gap.

Uncle Penn put his hands on his knees and pushed to
his feet. Beckoning Ray to follow, he led the way up
around the south corner of the house and up a little
avenue of redbud trees in bloom. Beyond the trees they
came out into a gently sloping field of knee-high grass,
rich golden-green in the late afternoon sun.

A few yards up into the meadow Ray stumbled
against a slab of stone and drew back, startled. "It's a
headstone!"

"Always headstones in a buryin' ground," Uncle Penn
observed, shuffling on. He waved a hand to take in the
whole of the field. "All the Twillys' Green folks're
here. All except your mama and some like young Delly's
brother Franklin who was killed in the wars Outside.
Here's the Dreegos, y'see?" He bent aside the grass that
hid one narrow upright stone so that Ray could read
the inscription:

ELIAS PENN DREEGO
Born 1833
Died 1953

A little further down the grassy row they came to

ELIM PENN DREEGO
1775
1912

Elim's father, Uncle Penn's great-grandfather, was not far beyond. The stone there read ELIS PENN-DREEGO 1715–1868. Beyond Mara, Elis's wife, and LYA—*Toke in Childhode by a gret Woolf,* Uncle Penn stopped to lay a hand on a blackened, lichen-spotted stone.

"This here's *his* daddy, my great-great."

Ray had to sit on his heels and lean close to make out the lettering.

ROB^T LILLICO

He Com in 1678

Age 23

Layd to Rest 1732

Ray frowned. "If he's Elis's father, how come his name's not Dreego?"

"The way I heerd it," Uncle Penn said, "they was kind of short of Dreegos just then. But the last one, he had a daughter and she married this Scotsman Lillico two-three years after he come. Injuns caught him down Carolina-way and brought him up along, but he got loose not far off and the Greeners they took him in. Anyhow, he didn't mind namin' their first son Penn Dreego to please the folk. Seems they'd always been a Dreego in the Green, and if they wasn't a born one handy, they just made them one. Always had to have a Watcher, I reckon."

Ray was only half attending. He moved back along the line of Dreegos laid out among their wives and children, working out the dates. They had to be wrong.

If Uncle Penn's father was born in 1833 and died in 1953, he would have been a hundred and twenty years old. The great-grandfather, Elis, would have been a hundred and fifty-three, and that was absurd. Impossible. Lillico, now, had died at seventy-seven. That was more reasonable.

Uncle Penn chuckled. "No, you done your sums right. Us Dreegos is long livers. What'd you say if I told you I re*mem*bered my great-granddaddy?"

"Him? The one who died in eighteen sixty-eight?" Ray's disbelief was obvious.

"That's the one." Uncle Penn cackled. "Makes me—let's see now—eighteen sixty-four makes me a hundred eleven year this year. I'll match my daddy easy, but us Dreegos since Lillico ain't a patch on the old days. 'Course, oncet upon a time *ever*body in the Green kept well, but sincet they all moved down-hollow, they ain't done so good. It's not just they never come back to the old ways. Air ain't so good down below as up here. I never did care for the feel of the Hollow, but if y' can't put your finger on just why, nobody pays any mind."

Ray tried to steer the old man back to his own concerns. "If they were Watchers, what did they *watch?* I mean, what do *you* watch. It's a funny thing to call anybody if they aren't really keeping watch over something."

Uncle Penn knocked the dottle from his pipe, tapping it carefully on a headstone, and then set about refilling it.

"Well, now, I don't know as I could say. I reckon it was just a name passed down along with 'Dreego.' Oh,

they was some old songs y' had t' learn, and some kinder
nonsense rhymes. Not a stick of it *meant* anything." He
lit a match and sucked at the pipe until he was wreathed
in a little cloud of fragrant smoke. Leaning his head
back and puffing thoughtfully, he said, "Seems to me
there was rules, too."

"Like in a game? Or for real?" Ray could hardly hide
his impatience. Songs and nonsense rhymes and mickey-
mouse "rules"? Not in the world of the Watchers he had
seen.

Uncle Penn considered. "They was all pretty com-
monsensical things, like 'Keep th' Hollow close from
strangers'; 'Grow in, wed in, stay in'; 'Keep the Watch
in the rockhouse well'; and 'Fell no tree till y' plant
another.' That sorta thing."

"I don't get it. What's there to watch in that old
rockhouse?" Still, Watchers had been there. It certainly
wasn't the Tûl Isgrun that Tekla's people were after, but
if that were close by. . . . The cave? Or the mine? But
no, there were people in and out of there all the time.

Uncle Penn shrugged. "If they was ever a reason, it's
long forgot."

Ray scuffed off through the grass, looking at tomb-
stones and trying to puzzle it all out. But there were too
many pieces missing.

In the far corner of the field there were stones that
appeared to be far older than those he had seen:
cylinders with domed tops, so weather-worn that only
on the leeward side could any carving be seen, and that
was blurred with lichen. Joining Ray by the first of

them, Uncle Penn opened up his clasp knife and scraped delicately at the lichen, cleaning out lines here and there until the whole of the remaining carving was revealed.

It might have been only a design, a decoration, but the repetitions were so irregular that they suggested some sort of writing: an inscription, half-obliterated. And the marks were very like those on the warning hand carved on the cave wall.

"Does this *say* something."

"Oh, it's writin' right enough. There's a whole box full of books with them kinder marks in 'em over to the Gare. Couldn't tell you what's in 'em, though." Uncle Penn shrugged. "Couldn't even if they's in reg'lar writin'. I never did learn t' read more'n enough to spell out the names when I got to carve a stone, like for poor Neva last month."

He chuckled a little at Ray's incredulous look. "Ain't just me. County schools didn't 'collect we was up here until thirty-forty years ago, and they had to start from scratch. Old Lillico, he taught th'English writin' to his boy, my great-granddaddy; and my granddaddy knew a good few of the words, but my daddy he had a time cipherin' out his own name."

"But you said there were *books*."

"Never knew a body who could read 'em. Oh I reckon somebody could oncet upon a time, or they wouldn't've got wrote. But they must've let their learnin' die on the vine. There's stones here 'thout any writin' atall." Uncle Penn pushed himself erect with a grimace. "Hoo! Gettin' a touch creaky in my middle age."

Ray scrambled up. "Look, this place the books are— what'd you call it?"

"The Gare. Think you'd like a look at 'em, eh? Got a real bee in your bonnet, ain't you? Well, come along. There's time before supper, and it's a right pretty walk."

It was, as Uncle Penn said, a "right pretty walk." From below, the dark beech and hemlock-browed ridges above the Hollow were both beautiful and forbidding, but once beyond the Dreego house and into the gardens and burying field, the forest climbed away east and west, for a broad wedge had been cleared through its middle to open a way for the sun. The fields, raggedy with neglect, climbed to the crest with apple orchards on either side as fences against the forest. The oldest apple trees, gnarled and bent, wore blossoms only in their topmost crowns, but the young trees spaced among them were heavy with bloom.

At the crest itself, Ray stopped to stare in wonder at

the land that fell away to form a wide and saucer-shallow valley tipped to catch the sun. Away to the south, the more familiar narrow-backed type of ridges faded into the gray-blue distance, but here was a high world apart, of fields and forest, hedge and garden, stretching perhaps two miles to the lower rim. Less than a hundred yards away, a stone house and barn sat, moss-covered, in the lee of an open wood of large maples, beeches, and oaks, looking as if they might have been there since before the great trees themselves.

The forest on this side of the gentle crest was no longer beech and hemlock, but red spruce and balsam; and even though it stood far off, the sweet fragrance of balsam hung in the air. It too was a dark forest, but where it fell away on the eastern side, great purple rhododendron thickets glowed under its eaves in the late sun.

Uncle Penn went ahead, pointing out landmarks. One particular oak was, he claimed, twenty feet taller and five more in girth than the famed Mingo Oak, which had been six hundred years old when it was felled in 1939. North beyond the dark forest, on the heights to the east and west of the Hollow, the land was "not much good," he explained. There the tree-girt uplands were bleak bogs rimmed with dogwood and fire cherry, and growing little of use but wild cranberries and the knotty, burly-rooted laurel that Uncle Penn like to carve for his briar pipe-bowls. "But this here's different." He made a wide sweep with his pipe-stem. "Drop a seed an' it's growin' pretty near soon as it hits the ground. Melons, all sorts of things that won't even sprout over on the other side. Like I tell Dream and them other young uns, it's purely crazy t' let a place like this here run to weed an' brush. Now, lookit that there. That's the old Mattick place."

The old Mattick place was even larger than the Dreego house, with a long low stone barn. Barn and house were joined by the wall that enclosed the barnyard, now full of rank grass and scrubby trees. If the house looked strangely familiar, Ray could not have said why, for it had more of a fairytale look than of something from any world he knew. Outside the walls, all that remained of the gardens were hedges run wild and the double rows of pear and peach trees that had lined the vanished walks.

Only the great walk had not vanished. From the front door of the old house, a wide stone-paved path led southward down an avenue of ancient tuliptrees. Seen from the ragged garden, they towered unbelievably tall, their new leaves glossy in the western sun and the blossoms all ablaze; but once upon the road itself, under that great, whispering vault of branches pillared by trunks twenty and more feet around, the old man and the boy walked in a deep and lovely gloom. And when they came to the bottom of the valley and the green arched way tipped upward, Ray saw the Gare at its far end.

It was a castle, perched among the dark and twisted Carolina hemlocks on the high valley's southern rim.

The Ruins

It was impossible to tell how large the ruin had once been, impossible even to tell whether it had been a fortress or a great huddle of dwellings, for the whole of it was covered with a tangle of flowering redberry, greenbrier, bitter nightshade, and creeping snowberry. The one circular tower still standing was wreathed in Virginia creeper, and near its foot, the broad leaves and browny-purple flowers of Dutchman's Pipe climbed among the vines. It might have been a grotesque, green-clad pillar of rock but for its door and the windows where the vines had been carefully pruned back.

Ray followed Uncle Penn out of the sweet gloom of the great aisle of tuliptrees and into a sea of brambles. Through its midst wound a path narrow as a deer-trail. The old man, and Ray behind him, edged along it sideways, crab-fashion, to avoid the thorns that plucked at shirts and trousers. Through an arch in one crumbling wall they came out onto a broad, mossy floor that might once have been a courtyard between rooms whose walls were now only hummocky lines of rubble under the blanket of green.

There were more stairs, leading down into other crumbled rooms and courtyards, and each broad tread was a long, single stone worn down in the middle with passing feet. Both the stairs and the right-hand balustrade had been kept clear.

"I trim it back 'bout oncet a month," said Uncle Penn to Ray's questioning look. "Them creepers can trip an old man up easy."

"It's not that—it's just . . . What *is* this place?" Ray was completely bewildered. The Gare was unbe*liev*able, and yet none of the cousins had said Word One about it. Let alone the fact that whatever it was, it no more belonged in the West Virginia mountains than a—a sailboat!

"It's just the Gare. That's all the name I ever heard. My granddaddy said there was Matticks still livin' over here when he was a tyke, with the place all tumbled down even then. Ain't much to look at, but a lot of us must've lived here oncet, seein' how it's so big." Looking around, he nodded regretfully. "It's good country, is

Up Top. Nothin's been much right sincet the folks moved down-Hollow.

"Looky here now," he said, as they came up to the tower. "Ain't nobody could lay stone like that nowadays." He stroked the wall next to the doorway with a veined hand and drew a finger along a joint so finely wrought that a knife-blade could not have been slipped between the dry-laid stones. "Artful old geezers they must've been."

Ray followed wordlessly into the cool dampness of a narrow entranceway. Last year he had dozed his way to a D in history class, and so his idea of what had happened where and when was shaky to say the least, but he was quite sure that a place like this had no business being here at all. If it were as old as it looked, it had to be Indian-built, but who ever heard of an Indian palace? In Mexico perhaps; but West Virginia? Besides, it had more the look of some of the European castles he had seen in old adventure films on TV. And even if there could be such a thing as a cross between a castle and an—an Inca palace, you wouldn't find it up here in the boondocks.

Uncle Penn indicated a narrow, steeply climbing stair on the left. "There y' go."

Ray went first, hurrying in spite of the dimness of the light let in by the narrow slitted windows spaced every few yards up the stairwell's curving course. The walls of the tower, it appeared, were double, with the stair climbing between them. Here and there on the right a window opened into the dark interior of the tower.

Passing them, Ray had the impression not of darkened rooms, but of emptiness, of a great hollow space.

At the top, the stairwell pierced a heavy oaken floor, emerging into a wide, round room. The room's thick walls were pierced all around its circuit with a series of tall, narrow windows—so many of them, so close together, that if half at least had not been obscured by the matted creeper, the effect would have been more like a circle of pillars than a wall. At the level of the windows' sills a stone bench carved with curious designs ringed the entire room. Some five or six feet in from this bench, toward the room's center, a circle of true pillars sprang to join the ribs of the tower's roof. Most astonishing of all, those stone ribs stopped short of the point toward which they soared, being joined together instead by a stone ring to form an opening about eighteen inches across. That opening had been filled with a great round stone, only roughly shaped, and gleaming dully in the leaf-green light. Below it, in the center of a broad expanse of floor, was an open well surrounded by a heavy wooden railing, richly carved: apparently a light-well into the room beneath.

It was almost too much to take in. Ray felt a little as if he'd had the wind knocked out of him. Dreams, it seemed, were no stranger than waking.

Uncle Penn, a little breathless from the climb, was enjoying Ray's amazement. "When you got somethin' like this . . . kinder makes sense keepin' strangers out, don't it? There was a professor-feller hung around Moars' a year or two ago, askin' a lot of questions 'bout the Hollow. Why, if he'd caught a whiff of this here, he'd've blatted it all over creation, and next thing you know, they'd say it was one of them 'historical mony-ments' and we'd no right to keep it hid. 'Fore you c'd spit, they'd 'doze them a highway straight up the moun-tain."

And run up a few gifty-shops and a Colonel Chicken's Barn, Ray thought. The Twillys' Greeners would end up weaving baskets of white oak splits and stitching quilts for the tourists. There was nothing really wrong with that, but somehow it made him shiver. The thought of this beauty and stillness shattered by the shrieks of small bored children and the satiny stone defaced by others, dismayed him. He had done that himself once, making a furtive scratchy *I-was-here* in a courthouse corridor in Apple Lock.

But not here. Never here.

"The books," he said, recovering himself. "You said there were books."

Uncle Penn came out of his own reverie by the western windows and pointed to a massive wooden chest by the centerwell railing. "There y'are. I'd best give a hand," he said, crossing to it. "Too heavy for one. I ain't had it open sincet one time three-four year ago when young Delly come up with me. Don't think any of the rest of 'em's ever been in it atall."

Ray, beside him, tugged at the massive lid shaped from a single great slab of oak. "But they all know about it, don't they? This place, I mean, and the books." He panted, straining at the lid.

"Unh. Mebbe not the young'uns." The lid swung heavily back against the rail. "They seem t' think Up Top's all bog, don't hardly come up to the house even, 'cept on errands. Harry and Roney used t' play up here 'round the Gare when they's little, but they steer clear of it now. Say the place gives 'em the creeps."

Ray drew a heavy cloth-wrapped oblong from the neatly-packed chest and with it a whiff of mothballs. "How come?"

"Purely nonsense. But young Delly comes now and again to give me a hand with them creepers. Let 'em go too long, and the dad-blamed things come crawlin' right in the windows and bring th' damp in with 'em. Can't have that."

Whoever had fashioned the great chest had also mistrusted the damp. The outer shell was lined with fragrant cedar, and that in turn with thin sheets of copper fitted snugly and lapped at the corners rather than nailed. It was filled almost full with linen-wrapped packages of various sizes. Some of the wrappings were richly embroidered, and others were marked with blurred and faded inks.

Ray unwrapped the one he held, finding beneath the layers of linen a box wrapped in a plastic bag bearing the legend *Garden-Fresh Produce*.

"Hah! Delly must've done that. Can't think when. Smells like mothballs too. Pretty good idea. I just been airin' 'em out every few year. Can't be too careful though. Mildew gets in, there's no gettin' rid of it."

The box was of some aromatic wood, polished, dark,

and sweet-smelling. The surface of the wood gleamed with strange designs, for the lines engraved in it had been set with tiny seed pearls to make a series of those same shapes he had seen on the gravestone, and in the cave:

The book inside the box was filled with masses of those same shapes. Here, though, there were varied colors, each used several times on any one page: wine-red, grass-green, jade-green, clear blue, in shifting combinations. It was pleasing to look at, but to Ray as meaningless as a scattering of colored tiddlywinks. "This can't really be writing," he protested.

"Looks as sensible as t'other kind to me," Uncle Penn observed.

To Ray's relief not all of the books turned out to be written in the strange word- or letter-shapes. One plain cotton cover had the name Lillico stitched on it and turned out to be a leather slipcase containing an old leather-bound diary about five inches wide and seven long. Both the book and its case had been stamped with the name *W. Buckland, Esq.*, but on both, this name had been scraped at and smoothed away until it was quite faint.

"Hey, this is more like it," Ray exclaimed, turning the pages. The diary was written not only in a proper alphabet, but in English. The entries on the first few pages were in a crabbed hand, difficult to read, and may have been some sort of business record for they included numbered lists that looked like inventories. These first pages had later been neatly crossed out, and the handwriting that followed was larger and considerably more readable. Some characters, like the small *s* that was in one place an *ſ* and in another more like a knot than a letter, were oddly shaped, but at least they could be puzzled out. The spelling, though, was even more peculiar than Ray's own. Only by careful, squinting attention was he able to make out the first sentence. Under the elaborately scrolled heading *Robt Allison Lillico*, it began *Le bon diew be thank^d th^t chance & murther hath mad mee a fre man in this yere of oure Lord 16 and 78.*

"Read hit aloud," prompted Uncle Penn. "I never knowed hit was an English book in that little case."

"I thought you said Delly came up here with you. If he put this in that plastic bag, he must've known. Can't *he* read?"

"Delly's a nice boy," Uncle Penn said, "and strange or no, he's a hard worker. But I doubt he's much of a hand at readin'. You go ahead, boy."

It was not easy. Lillico's tale unwound slowly, beginning as an account of past adventures and then becoming a journal, each year's entry shorter than the last, of life on the highlands above Twillys' Green Hollow.

A Scot, Robert Lillico had come to America as the indentured servant of William Buckland—the crossed-out entries had been his—a Virginia gentleman intent on finding a passage across the western mountains. On his second attempt to reach those mountains, Buckland was, like the explorer Needham before him, murdered by the Occaneechees. Lillico, escaping, was picked up by a tribe of the Tamahita and taken along, half-prisoner and half-comrade, on their raids across the Carolina border and up to the Ohio headwaters. Escaping again, and believing it far safer to follow a stream down to the coast rather than to strike out across the dense forest, he had doggedly followed a sizable creek for miles before it unexpectedly turned north. At the same time he spied the smoke from the Tamahitas' evening campfire behind him. There was nothing to do but follow north downstream. The French were somewhere to the north, and the French and Scots were old allies; so from dawn the next morning he followed the stream deeper into the wilderness.

On the fifteenth day after his escape, Lillico avoided running into a band of Cherokees moving upstream only by striking out blindly to the west, cross-country. He was half-starved, for though he had managed to steal his own rifle away from the Tamahita, he had been wary of shooting any game for fear of bringing more savages down upon him. Weakened by hunger and the terrors of being alone in a boundless forest, he grew rash and fell, attempting a rocky slope too steep for his strength. One of the Watchers, out hunting, had found him before the wolves or pumas did.

These are a strange folk & no mystake. They call themselfs WATCHERS but noe not w^t they watch. Strangest of alle som wordes in theyr tong are very like the Galic. From the fyrst I have ben able to make myself understode to them. I thot some Welchman had got in amongst them but they say they have spoken so sence their people com to this place. Th^t is some tyme gone, for the fortress has the loke of gret age.

They say further th^t now I have com I may not goe, but I had not thot of going. Ther is a fayre yong woman here, daughter to one of their gret men. They are dark skinned alle, with the hye cheke-bones of the Indians, but with lite blue eyes or grey, which is a gret oddity in this land and a mystery. Ther is one lad with reddish hair, which lokes uncommon strange. In the blue embroydered cloaks they wear . . .

Uncle Penn, sitting on the window-bench, interrupted, nodding enthusiastically. "That girl now, she'd be Perela, my great-great-grandma."

Going on, Ray skimmed over much of the account, which included a description of Up Top, the Hollow, and the game—deer and bear, occasionally elk and buffalo. Uncle Penn wouldn't know the difference, and Ray, though he began to despair of it, kept hoping that Lillico was going to discover something about Tûl Isgrun or the reason for the Watch. In 1687 he recorded the deaths from smallpox of half the settlement on the heights. One of the huntsmen, miles from home, had stopped to give water to a dying Cherokee abandoned by his companions and had brought back news that a great epidemic was raging among the upland tribes. He brought the pox with him as well.

From 1700 on, Lillico more and more often noted reports of traders and explorers probing into the mountains, skirting the ridges to the south. The huntsmen among the Watchers had been used to traveling long distances, secretly learning much of the movement of men and tribes, but after 1715 they clung more closely to their own high hills.

It was at about this time—though the first actual mention of it was in 1730—that Lillico began the translation of "a curious boke in the Latin tong," which he had discovered among the volumes in the tower. The journal entries continued, however, to relate the everyday round of life: births, deaths, and the occasional coming of an outlander who could not be turned away. There were several—an exhausted runaway slave, an English child escaped from Occaneechee marauders, and a lame Cherokee girl abandoned by companions fleeing a Tamahita slaving party. In 1732 the journal was taken over by a new hand—Uncle Penn's great-grandfather, apparently—and the entries became even more brief. The entire entry for 1788 read: *Downland hunters sey settlers find th gap 3 dayes west. Thes men are gret cutters of trees & wastfull butchers of game. We must be as shadowes now.*

Uncle Penn was no longer attending. His eyes were on the stairwell, and he listened, frozen, birdlike. "Hark a minute," he cautioned. "Hear that?"

"Hear what?" Ray riffled through the rest of the book, looking for something that might be the translation Lillico had spoken of. It was not there. After the last entry, in 1852, the pages all were blank. The only indication that there might have been something was that at the very back a number of sheets had been neatly sliced out, leaving a narrow tell-tale stub.

"There 'tis again," Uncle Penn whispered. Snatching Ray's hand, he pulled him across to the nearest pillar and laid it against the stone. "Feel that?"

A faint vibration rose in the pillar, pulsing stronger and then slowly dying away.

Ray backed off. "What is it? An earthquake?"

"I dunno," the old man answered with a scowl. "Never felt such a thing before. Can't say I much like bein' perched atop this rockpile while it's doin' it, neither. Here, stick that book away and come along."

The second tremor hit as they reached the bottom of the long stair.

"Wow!" Ray was wide-eyed. "That feels *weird*."

"I don't like it *at*all," Uncle Penn declared firmly. "We'd best get back to the house 'fore Mavee gets to frettin'."

They had gone about a half mile along the darkening tree-lined path when they were greeted by a loud *Halloo!* from ahead. A moment later Ray made out Uncle Dream striding along, with old Aunt Mavee puffing determinedly behind.

"Praise be you're all right, you silly old man," Aunt Mavee gasped out as she came up. She held one hand pressed to her side. "You've give me a stitch from hur-ryin'. We was sure that old Gare'd come down on your head."

"Did you feel it down in the Hollow, too?" Ray was surprised that Uncle Dream could have made it up so fast.

Uncle Dream looked his vaguest and most perplexed. "I dunno. Our old Flower-bitch didn't come along home for her supper, so I was kind of lookin' around for her up here. I was over visitin' with Aunt Mavee when it come."

"Blamed if it didn't rattle every slate on the roof," Aunt Mavee put in. "When it come the second time, I *knew* you was in that dreadful old tower. I said to Dream—"

Uncle Dream put out his hand to interrupt. "It just come to me. I'll bet you they're blastin' over in one of the far hollows. They do say the coal comp'ny's openin' up a new seam over the other side of Muddy. Mebbe I'll go along minward and have a look-see. You want to come along, boy?"

Aunt Mavee observed tartly that they would have to hurry to be back before dark, and so Uncle Dream set off at what was for him a sharp pace, leaving the Dree-gos heading homeward to pen their chickens up for the night.

By "minward" Uncle Dream apparently meant toward a vantage point along the rim of the Up Top highland from which they could see out across the neighboring ridges and valleys. After a good mile's walk, first through scrubby woods that had once been cultivated fields and then skirting a high boggy area Uncle Dream called "the Miggen," they came to a great outcrop of rock looking out to the east and north. Below its sheer sides the hill fell away into Moon Hollow at so steep an angle that its trees were stunted from the effort of keeping their scant foothold.

"There! Something's going on down there." Ray pointed.

At the far bottom of Moon Hollow, quite a way distant, a small cavalcade of equipment rigs, trucks, pickups, and cars wound downward out of sight. The hollow itself was naked, shorn of trees, and what shacks still stood gaped eyeless and abandoned.

One last truck pulled away from the coal-tipple loading dock midway up the hollow. The small knot of men standing there gave a cheer as a diesel engine came tooting out of the mine's drift entrance. The men in the cars behind it spilled out and went pouring down the stairway by the tipple. The engine driver veered his equipment down the dangerously steep slope beside it and gained the bottom before them in a cloud of dust. There was a confusion of shouting, and as Ray and his uncle watched, the men raced for the opposite side of Moon Hollow, waded across the little creek, and clambered up the stony hillside.

The mountain shook again, this time wracked with a visible shudder. The shock, almost on the instant, rocked the outcrop where Ray and Uncle Dream stood, so that they stepped quickly back, alarmed that they might be shaken over the edge, lookout and all. Then, as they watched, Moon Ridge—the long thick-middled spur that formed the northern wall of Moon Hollow—seemed to shift, to blur, and then, horribly, to settle. The trees along its crest lurched drunkenly. Patches of hillside slid downward, trees and earth and undergrowth together, raising a great, slow dust on the bare lower slopes.

The mine opening gave a monstrous belch of black dust and then dissolved.

The Watcher in the Trees

"Lordy," breathed Uncle Dream. "I've heard of bringin' a mine clean, but that's somethin' else again. I'll bet them fellows up on the hill won't ever want them a closer shave than that!"

When his astonishment died down a little, he explained that "bringing it clean" meant taking out the last possible ton of coal, a delicate and often dangerous business. Like most of the deep mines in Withers County, the Moon mine had started as a little one- or two-man mine back before the forties and grown from there. In the years up until its closing in 'forty-eight, it

had become a two-level giant, honeycombed with galleries that crept as close as safety allowed to the mountain's outer wall. The ridge itself was held up like a
monstrous roof only by the massive pillars of coal sepa-
rating the galleries.

In the old truck-mine days pillars were considered
lost coal. They remained when the mines petered out
and were closed down. But when big mine operators
moved in, replacing mine ponies with conveyor belts and
diesel engines, there was, at least in theory, a chance to
"bring it clean" when the seams were finally worked out.
This meant robbing the furthest pillars of the main
seam, pulling back in shuttle cars and the "coal moles"
so that on their last trip out to the mine entrance the
machines could cut through the pillars, leaving the great
roof to crash behind them. The seam being worked in
Moon Ridge since the reopening of the mine had been
the thickest yet—eight feet—and that would have meant
quite a roof-fall even if there had not been two other
levels supported by dangerously skimpy pillars.

"Them old levels was the Top Hole Number Two
mine your granddaddy and Cloyce and Harry worked
in. I was only there toward the end. It's took a long
whiles to work the old ridge out. That'll be why they're
movin' over past Muddy—and why I got this here
letter."

He pulled a folded envelope from his hip pocket and
drew the letter from it. Pointing a grimy finger at the
symbol on the letterhead, he said "I know
that's the coal comp'ny, and I kin make out it's about a

job, but I couldn't find Rainelle to read it out clear to me. Here, you got enough light to make it out by?"

Ray smoothed the paper out against his knee and then tilted it to catch the waning light. "It's from the Deep Run Coal Company in Williamson," he said, and read out:

Dear Mr. Clewarek:

As a former employee of Top Hole Mine No. 2 of the former Ridge Mining Company, now a division of Deep Run Coal Company, you may be interested to hear that we will be opening two new mines, Top Holes No. 3 and 4, on or about June first. In view of our policy of whenever possible employing local and experienced men, we will be pleased to see you at the Elks Hall in Willocks on May 23, where we will be taking applications for forty new jobs.

> *Yours sincerely,*
> *E.P. Faussett,*
> PERSONNEL MANAGER

Uncle Dream snorted. "Pretty fancy. They used to just stick a notice up down to Moars' and tell old Arbie to pass the word. When'd it say? Two weeks from Friday? Guess I'll have to go along down. Funny they don't say where the work'll be, though."

Tuesday morning was bright, promising a warm day, but in spite of the weather and the prospect of work— Ad Tullo and Roney Yanto had also had letters—the mood of the Hollow was uneasy. The Clewareks' bitch Flower had been found late the night before, dead in the brush high up the creek. She had been badly mauled, and Dream reported unhappily that it looked almost like a mountain lion's work, even though there were no tracks to show it, and none had been seen in the hills for years. He warned Aunt Star to keep Mary-Mary and Jody close in, in case some large animal were hanging around. June Ann was so upset about Flower that her mother said she might stay home from school if she helped with the little ones.

Aunt Star fussed over Ray too. "Don't them stitches make your head ache?"

Startled, Ray touched the bandage. He had actually forgotten it. "No, it's O.K. Anyhow, I got to look up something in that school library, so I might as well go in. And you don't need to fix me any lunch. I got some money for the cafeteria."

Loping down the path ahead of Rainelle, he grinned to himself. Imagine needing an excuse to go to school! Truth to tell, he was actually looking forward to a school lunch, and that was funny too. Yesterday's sight of wafer-thin hamburgers and fruit-jello salad had made him long for a change from his aunt's pale beans, biscuits with pale pork gravy, and bland syrup-soaked corn bread. It was no wonder the Hollow kids looked so pasty, despite their dark skin. They *were* pasty.

Bob-White and Dawn caught up just above Yantos'. "You hear?" Bob-White asked with morbid excitement. "Our dog Bill, he got hisself kilt. Grandma found him this mornin'. She says a varmint got him."

"Poor old Bill." Little Dawn mourned.

Bob-White nodded, solemn and knowing. "Grandma says it ain't just Saturday nights any more. There's somethin' stirrin' all the time."

Ray felt as suddenly, icily cold as if he had just stepped into the creek. "Where'd she find him?" he said.

"Up in them bushes 'twixt our house and that old cave."

Rainelle shivered. "It got our Flower too."

Bob-White nearly skipped in his excitement. "Honest? When we come past Uncle Harry's, Delly he said Tullos' Yellow Rose was under the house this mornin' and wouldn't come out for nothing."

The puzzle deepened at Yantos', where Merle waited by the path with more grim news. Patches, the meanest dog in the Hollow, had been found half in and half out of the creek—not drowned and not a mark on him, but with "the scaredest look I ever did see," as Merle put it.

"Cut that out," Ray said angrily. "You're giving the baby the creeps." Dawn *was* clinging suspiciously close to Rainelle and looking very wide-eyed.

"C'mon or we'll miss the bus," Rainelle said, dragging Dawn after her. Ray, on the way down, was treated to Merle's theories, one being that Patches had been "squoze" to death. But when asked "by what?" his imagination dried up.

Ray's had not. To his own mild surprise, Ray was thinking. He had been doing it off and on for a day and a half, and it was an oddly pleasant sensation. "Oddly," because it was not about anything pleasant. The puzzle of Twillys' Green's past looked like intruding itself on Twillys' Green's present in a distinctly unpleasant fashion.

Something, he knew, was wrong: both in Hoop Hollow and in the uneasiness that came over Twillys' Green at dusk. And though it seemed crazy, he was convinced that it had something to do with his "dream" and the Watcher in the cave. The Watchers were at the center of it all. But at the center of what? If Tekla's Tûl Isgrun *was* in Twillys' Green and was what the Watchers guarded . . .

Tûl Isgrun . . . *Tuh-lees-gruh-n* . . .

Twillys' Green! It was the old name of something *in* the Hollow, not the Hollow itself And what in the Hollow could be watched from the rockhouse but the approach to the cave? Tekla had been drawn there because of Ruan; and if Ray had thought it strange to walk in the other boy's skin, he was suddenly frightened to think how well that skin might fit.

For he had drawn Arbie Moar.

And he did not know what it was all about.

To make a bad day worse, the school lunch turned out to be a sticky mess of Spanish rice with bits of chopped frankfurter in it. And the library had no books on castles or forts. Their only picture-encyclopedia, an out-of-date *Source Book*, had a short article on castles that would have been unhelpful no matter why you happened to be interested. And Miss Powe hadn't heard from her brother about the old Indian mound city near

Charleston. It probably wasn't old enough to be Tekla's Kanhuán anyway.

On the way home, Moars' Store was full of grim faces and a-buzz with news of the death Monday afternoon in Moon mine of someone named Billy Jim Boddie. Some of the muttering among the groups of men on the front porch was ugly. Local 7890 had come out on strike because, as one story had it, a foreman had miscounted the number of men coming out of the mine—or the number that had gone in earlier—and that the pull-back klaxon had sounded only once, and then not for long. Billy Jim was a little deaf; just deaf enough to miss it. So now Billy Jim had a whole mountain for a tombstone.

" 'Pull 'em all out in one move, big equipment first,' " somebody quoted bitterly. " 'Cut the man-hours.' Deep Run Coal's got the worst safety record in the state, but they don't say 'Cut the accident rate.' Hell, no! 'Cut the man-hours.' "

Inside, Ray bought two cans of soft drink and hurried out again, but there was Arbie Moar's broad back ahead of him, and Arbie shaking his head gravely and saying, "We'll miss old Billy Jim around here. Why, when Mutch was laid up last year with the flu, Billy Jim he came along Saturdays to give me a hand in the storage shed. A good man."

Ray and three of the Twillys' Green children—Merle always hitched a ride up to the Corners after baseball practice—were across the road and opening the cans to share around on the long walk when Arbie caught sight of them and called, "Whoa up there a minute, Mister

Siler! You thought any more on that little matter we talked about?"

"Naw. Forgot to ask," Ray yelled back. He shrugged awkwardly and plodded on. Maybe Mr. Moar would decide he was a bit thick in the upstairs, and let the whole thing drop. That stone snake—he still didn't know how that first scrap ever got in his pocket.

Once around the bend and out of sight, Ray pulled from his pocket the three letters Bonnie had given him when he paid for the pop. One was for Ad, one was for Dream, and one was his own—from his father. *Dear Ray* said the cramped handwriting huddled near the top of a piece of Aura Lee's flowered writing paper:

> Well, you got Aura Lee and the girls stirred up real good like you figured, so I guess you get another chance. But youd best understand. I talked to the school principal and Judge Kraft. I have really had it with you. One more lick of trouble and I swear Ill pack you off to juvenal court. You think on that and come home cheerful. You be useful to Aura Lee and do good in school and well see.
>
> Dad

Stapled in the lower left-hand corner was the precious bus ticket.

Ray folded the letter thoughtfully and replaced it in the envelope. It took a while for it to sink in. He'd got what he wanted. He'd got what he wanted, but all he could think of was "Later, maybe. Not now."

Rainelle handed over the half-empty can. "Your folks O.K.?"

Ray took a long swallow and finished it off. He wiped his mouth with the back of his hand. "Yeah." He tossed the can to the side of the road and then flushed when Rainelle went back to pick it up.

"Delly, he makes pretty things out of the tin," she explained apologetically. "For on Christmas trees."

Delly. He was another thing. Somebody—Delly's dad?—had said he kept an eye on the kids on the way home from school when Merle wasn't along. Maybe he kept an eye on Bonnie too. It *could* have been Delly he saw slipping along the hillside that first afternoon. He was a funny bird. And in thick with Uncle Penn, too.

Absently, Ray thrust the letter from his father into his pocket. Apple Lock seemed a world away.

Hey there!

Ray looked up to see that Rainelle and Bob-White and Dawn had drawn well ahead. Just beyond them, below the point where the dirt road branched up into Horse Hollow, three huge earth-movers were pulled up at the side of the road.

"Hey, pretty girl! C'mon, give us a smile."

The drivers and two other men lounged against one of the monster tires on the first machine, grinning.

Rainelle, head down, her books clutched in one arm and little Dawn held fast by the hand, hurried on. Bob-White held his ground, but uncertainly, unsure whether to dash after the girls or wait for Ray. Ray broke into a run, but before he reached the first of the great yellow machines, the teasing catcalls stopped abruptly.

The men did not see Ray. They stared upward at something or someone on the hillside above the Horse Hollow turnoff. Slowing, Ray peered upward to see what they were staring at, and when he saw, he drew back behind the rear machine. The men, who had moved out into the middle of the road, were an ugly lot, large and ill-featured. One beckoned mockingly to the tall figure shadowed among the trees.

"Come along down, bogey-man. Let's have a look at you."

The figure did not move, but stayed at rest: a tall, shadowy shape, somehow threatening in its waiting silence. After a moment the man who had spoken backed off, shrugging his shoulders in pretended unconcern. With a cocky word to the others, he ambled around to the far side of his grader to sit on the grassy verge. When his companions joined him, Ray returned to the road and caught up with Bob-White. The girls were out of sight up around the bend, and the figure on the hillside had melted into the trees.

They came up to the girls just after the Hoop Hollow turnoff. "You O.K.?" Ray asked Rainelle. "They scare you?"

"I'm O.K.," she said. "But it was kind of scary. It— it wasn't *friendly*, like teasing."

Ray tried to sound unconcerned "I guess they didn't mean any harm. Do you know, I bet that road equipment means that one of those new mines is going to be up in Horse Hollow."

He talked on, meaninglessly, his mind racing. It had

been Delly there in the woods. Delly, but not the Delly he had figured for such a rabbit that first night, nervous, hunched up, staring off into nowhere or into the shadows of his own mind. He had been unmistakable enough just now in his faded plaid flannel shirt and the old army fatigue trousers Aunt Luce had tried with small success to dye a berry-brown. But there the resemblance ended. He was bigger than Ray had thought, but it wasn't that. When Uncle Dream straightened up he was tall, too, but Uncle Dream would never be anything more than a big, nice man. Delly, now . . .

Delly had stood in the shadows, tall, raven-haired, the gray eyes almost silver in that gloom, unmoving. It was as if his silence gathered to it other shadows, other hillsides, a sense of ancient power: vibrant but stilled, leashed, but still frightening. *Elzevir* . . .

And with that name out of nowhere, Ray knew. If there were still a Watcher, it was Delly. Not Uncle Penn, perched Up Top, but Delly, down in the shadows.

Delly

After supper Adney came up to the Clewareks' and sat at the table with Dream, puzzling over the letters Ray had brought. Both were from Cooper, Pilwell, and Smalley, attorneys-at-law in Taggert, the county seat. They asked Ray to read out Dream's again, and when he had, Adney nodded.

"Yuh, that's just what Sue Ellen made this'n out to say."

The letter served notice that on the next day, Wednesday, Mr. T. J. Pilwell would meet with the subsidiary legatees of Mrs. Divendly Viana Tullo "in order to inform them of the disposition of her estate," and would they please present themselves for a reading of the will at two o'clock in the afternoon.

"Divendly Viana?" said Rainelle with a giggle, looking up from the fingering she had been practicing on her guitar. "Who's *that*?"

"That was Ma." Adney smiled. "She couldn't stand it neither. Called herself Neva from the time she was a kid."

"What I'd like to know," Uncle Dream growled, "is what's a legatee?"

Nobody knew.

Ray, for his part, didn't much care. He still had his own puzzle: Tûl Isgrun. It just might be something to do with that Black Wall in the mine. A "shrine," that was what Tekla had called it. Well, weren't shrines usually decorated up? What if the snake were not a fossil at all, but a carving? Or was something that three-dimensional called a sculpture? Anyway, the cleft in the hill had been there long before the mine, so there *might* have been some sort of shrine back in there. But having arrived at that conclusion, Ray felt no wiser than before. Tomorrow he would try for another look at that snake. Just now he had other plans.

There was still an hour or so before dark. Ray picked up his rolled-up jacket and the two books he'd brought from school and drifted unnoticed out onto the front porch. But instead of settling down to homework, a minute later he was racing for the Up Top path.

Ray was breathless by the time he reached the top of the Gare tower stair. He had slipped past Dreegos', not wishing to drag over at Uncle Penn's slow pace. The old man wouldn't mind. And if he did? Ray felt an unaccustomed compunction. Maybe he ought to stop by on the way back—say he'd closed the books up good and tight. Last night they hadn't even shut the lid down.

The Latin book mentioned in Lillico's journal turned up at the very bottom of the great chest: twenty-five or so closely-written sheets of stiff deerskin parchment, wrapped in a coarse dark blue fabric. But there was no sign of Lillico's translation in that parcel or elsewhere.

Ray settled himself on the bench by the western windows with the manuscript and the two books he had brought from the school library. One was *Using Latin*, and the other a much-thumbed old Latin dictionary. He had only the vaguest idea of how to go about using them, but he meant to have a stab at it. And it was no go. The handwriting was almost as indecipherable as the characters in the other books and sprinkled through with squiggles and curlicues. A word that might have been *serpens*—serpent?—appeared on several pages, but otherwise there seemed to be very few complete words at all. Ray, disgusted, supposed that the squiggles at the ends of groups of letters, and perched above others, were either some private code or perhaps a system of abbreviations. In the end he could make out only two additional words, and those not only because they appeared in red in a margin beside the underlined notation *A.D. CCCXXX*, but because they were familiar: *Tûl Isgrun.* "Good old Twillys' Green again," he muttered.

"Aye, Twillys' Green. Sounds a nice, friendly name,

don't it?" The quiet voice came from the shadows at the top of the stairs.

"*Who's that?* Delly?"

Delly moved across the darkening room to reach down and turn the manuscript pages to the last one. There, delicately drawn, was the hoop snake, tail-in-mouth like those in the cave and mine, but here the center was inked in, making it a black disc held in the serpent's circle.

Below it a warning hand was lightly sketched, like that in the cave, along with what might have been an explanation of the strange characters on it.

"But what does it *mean?*"

Delly did not answer for a moment. " 'Tûl Isgrun'? I suppose you could say it means 'shrine of darkness.' A nice, friendly name. Anyways, it seems to've stuck to us one way or another." He gave an uneasy glance toward the windows and the darkening sky and, looking out across the treetops spreading below, frowned, as if he could see beneath to the shadows gathering at their feet. Without turning, he said, "Best pack the books away. I come along on purpose to bring you down. It ain't good to be out past dark with cougars and such on the prowl."

Ray moved to the chest. "You think it was a cougar

got the dogs, then?" He began stacking the books inside.

"Might be. Must've been, the way the two of them was mauled. It's queer, though. Uncle Penn says there's not been a one around here in fifty years. And they ain't the half of it. There's been signs of foxes and weasels, a lot of 'em, mostly around toward the Miggen. A regular convention of varmints. I don't like it atall. Too much goin' on to keep an eye on it all."

Ray retrieved his schoolbooks and jacket. He stuck the flashlight that had been rolled up in the jacket into a pocket and turned to follow his cousin, who was now only a tall shadow in the gloom. Odd that Delly could seem as nervous and self-effacing as ever, and yet . . . well, reassuring. "How come you know about Tûl Isgrun when nobody else does?"

Delly started down the steps ahead of him. "Me? I don't know much. Uncle Penn's daddy taught me a deal of things, but I was only seven when he died. No tellin' why he picked me. Look, you mind walkin' instead of talkin'? I want to get back down-Hollow quick as we can. I come straight here from over Hoop way. Seemed to me there was somethin' funny stirrin' over there and I'd best make sure everybody was safe home."

The darkness fell swiftly when it came, and in the thick night under the tuliptrees the flashlight was more than welcome. Ray was still full of questions, but neither Delly nor the darkness were very encouraging, so he trotted along in silence. They were halfway to Dreegos' before Ray said abruptly, "What'd Aunt Neva Tullo die *of* if everybody here lives so long?"

Delly slowed his pace. "Aunt Neva? Guess she wasn't

old as some, but Ad had her to a doctor down in Willocks a time or two. Some kind of heart ailment. Why?"

"I dunno . . ."

Delly seemed to debate with himself, and when he spoke, it was reluctantly. "No sense givin' the kids a fright, so we all kept quiet. Happened on a Saturday night. She went out alone with a pail of apple parings for Ad's hogs and keeled over with a heart attack. But something give her a terrible start, I'd say, from the look on her."

Ray was startled. "Uncle Dream didn't say . . ."

"It happened a whiles before the varmint killings—Erla's calf and Aunt Mavee's hens and them. Pa says we got more varmints because last winter was so hard everywheres else they all come here." But Delly was clearly unconvinced.

"Has it got something to do with whatever's wrong down in that cave-place—the Hole?"

Delly stopped still. "How do you mean, 'wrong'?"

The whole story spilled out: the discovery of the stone serpent, the dream and encounters, everything. Delly said nothing, but looked more and more troubled. For a long moment afterward there was only the faint sound of their footsteps.

"Mebbe," Delly said at last, "mebbe there still is something there, down at the roots of the mountain, that's meant to stay there. There's an old song . . .

> *From the broken shrine*
> *Darkness spreads across the hills,*
> *Fills the valleys*

And the hearts of men.
Our kindred are fled beneath the moon,
And we are left among the ruins."

"That makes it sound like it *was* broken," Ray said. "But then there'd be nothing there now."

Delly turned, a disturbing, daunting presence at the light's edge. Though he could not see it, Ray felt himself held in that strange, pale gaze. There seemed to be two Dellys—or rather, one like a candle flame wavering and guttering in an unseen wind that now and again sprang suddenly tall and clear. One moment he was as unsure as Ray himself, and in the next . . . "Not much for questions, are you?" Delly said. "Well, just now mebbe I'm not much for answers. You coming?"

When they came to the head of the trail leading down into Twillys' Green, a lamp gleamed faintly in the Dreegos' parlor window nearby. Below, in the Hollow of the Green, six pricks of light glimmered in the deep pool of darkness.

Delly stood silhouetted against the lamplight, hunched and tense, the old Delly again. "L-listen!" he whispered.

Ray listened, but he heard nothing more than an owl-hoot far off and a thin thread of music winding up from someone's TV.

"You hear it?" came Delly's nervous whisper. "The hum?"

"No. But it sure is dark down there." Even as he watched, the points of light seemed to soften and grow more obscure.

Delly drew him back from the edge and into the lee of Aunt Mavee's hen house. "When I was over to Hoop," he said worriedly, "they was having a meeting. No cars. Just the Hoop folk. It was a peculiar hour to be having a service, so I clumb up on the woodpile and watched through that high back window. Well, they was singing. Not words—just a high kind of wavery hum, with six or seven of 'em kneeling in a circle, moving like they was one creature . . ." Delly's voice shook slightly, but whether with remembered fear or indignation, Ray could not tell. "I had a feeling whatever it was they was calling down, I didn't want to be there when it lit."

Ray snorted rudely. "Fiddling around with snakes isn't very churchy to start with."

"Well, now, I guess I go along with Pa on that," Delly said consideringly. "There's ways and ways. It's kind of a desperate way to get comfort, but some seem to need it. But this was something else again, like—like they was being emptied out. I once saw a hypnotist do that in one of them clubs in Saigon. He had these three G.I.s and a big old dog and a pretty little Viet gal all doing that: swaying away in some kind of hollow dream. It give me the creeps then, too."

Ray shifted uneasily.

"You sure you don't hear nothing?" Delly asked again. "Well, come along down, then. Star'll be nervous as a cat, your being out on your lonesome in the dark. I get a little spooked myself without them dogs around. That old Yellow Rose hasn't come out from under Ad's house yet."

Ray groped his way carefully. The path was difficult in broad daylight; in the blind darkness it was downright alarming. The flashlight was no help because he needed both hands free. In several places the track was so narrow that you couldn't set one foot beside the other, and so he went cautiously. A few yards down he stopped and leaned against a jutting rock to take the books from under his arm and loosen his belt a couple of notches so that he could stuff them inside his waistband at the back. Then, gingerly, he turned to work his way down the nasty part. How did old Uncle Penn ever manage?

Delly was waiting at the bottom, and together they took the path that led past the old deserted house down to Clewareks'. Without the flashlight and the dim bluish light in the front window, Ray was convinced that not even sure-footed Delly would have found it. It was that dark. Not a star or scrap of moon.

"It's like walking around in a bowlful of ink. How're you going to get across the creek to your place? You want this?" Ray held out the flashlight.

"I can see a little." Delly's voice was distant, a little vague, as if he were still listening to the darkness. Then he recalled himself. "Look here—if ever you need come fetch me for anything, best way is to wade across. That way you got the plank for a railing."

And he was gone. But sounds were deceptive at night, Ray thought, as he stepped up onto the porch. Delly's soft footfalls seemed to move down toward Tullos' and not across to the creek. Down at Tullos' Yellow Rose whined piercingly.

"Ray?" Aunt Star opened the door and peered out through the sagging screen. "That you, honey? Thank heavens!" Then, nodding toward the unhappy sound coming from the dog down at Tullos', she said, "I don't see how Opal and Sue Ellen stand it. That galaroosing's worse'n having no dogs atall. Here, c'mon in before you catch your death. It's turned real chill out, hasn't it?"

The children made room for Ray at the best end of the old sofa, but he found the snowy blurs of *Hawaii Five-O* almost impossible to watch. He was concerned about Delly. Besides, he could tell from the dialogue that the show was a rerun of an old Wo Fat episode he had already seen.

Aunt Star dozed in the rocker. Uncle Dream and the girls were glued to the television, but Ray several times caught himself dropping off to sleep even in mid-gun-shot. After the third time the picture seemed darker and clearer, though the sound was garbled past understanding. He saw that someone lay on the ground. Two others knelt over him. When he saw that the soot-grimed one lying in the dry grass was himself, he thought muzzily, "Got to wake up," but he could not. He watched the nearer kneeling figure turn a sooty, tear-runnelled face to the other and speak again. The words lagged, as if they came to him through thick layers of cotton. *Warn Elzevir . . . the Gare . . . you and he are last of the First, and they are seeking out the paths to find you. . . .*

The other stood. Ray saw that she was dark and bitter-beautiful, young and old and ageless. She ran like a deer across the moon-silver field, but dark shapes that crouched at the top of the trail from the Hollow saw her and followed.

Elzevir?

Ray's head came up with a jerk as his elbow slipped from the sofa-arm. *Delly*, he thought, without knowing why. *Warn Delly* ...

Intruders

Yellow Rose was quiet, and the porch light at the lower Tullo house shone dimly. Ray found Delly there, having a word with Adney.

"Suit yourself," Adney was saying. He shrugged. "But if I was you I'd step down to Roney's and fetch Merle. That boy, he could pick off a wildcat with a .22. Anyhow, you take care." The door squeaked shut.

Delly did not seem surprised at Ray's reappearance, and made no objection to his tagging along. He skirted up behind Adney's, Uncle Roy's house, heading down-hollow along the top of the cornfield—or so Ray, following blindly, supposed. Delly had warned him against using the flashlight. They stopped at the bottom of the field, where a fallen tree made a makeshift bench above the pond, overlooking the pond and the road beyond it. They could hear the water in the spillway where the creek poured down out of the Hollow.

Some of the darkness must have poured out with it. Ray could see a little now, faintly, and a few bright stars had appeared.

"Watch it there!"

The words hissed across the water from somewhere below. Delly's hand fastened on Ray's wrist in warning. Above the sound of the sliding creek came footfalls, the faint scrape of boots against stone, a soft, heavy *pad-pad* on the wooden bridge.

"Four of 'em." Delly breathed. He slipped down along the field's edge with Ray close behind.

"Hadn't we ought to roust out Cousin Roney and Merle?" Ray whispered. The Yanto house was closest.

"Let's see what they're up to first."

A faint light that must have been a covered flashlight sprang up on the far hillside. "They've gone up that little side branch," Delly murmured. "Now I wonder what for. Nothing up there but Dream's old sweet-corn patch and a lot of briers."

A second light appeared, as they watched, and moved downward, followed by the first. They wavered for a moment and then turned up-Hollow along the hillside, keeping well above the Mattick and Lillico houses and outbuildings. Lightless, Delly and Ray kept abreast, moving along the west bank of the creek. Starlight drifted down into the hollowed hills, but for anyone who did not know the ground as well as Delly it was too little to help. Only because he could hear the water could Ray make out the darker shadow that was the creek.

The lights opposite jiggled on as before, poking here and there in the brush, now and again moving up the slope, and then drawing down toward the straggling barbed-wire fences. There was a light on at Matticks', but at Erla and Cloyce's all was dark. At the plank bridge across the creek, Delly signed to Ray to take off his shoes, removing his own boots and knotting the laces so that he could sling them around his neck. He led the way, stepping into the cold, rushing water and easing across, guided by the plank.

On the far side Delly hung his boots on a fencepost, but Ray had to stop to put his shoes on again. Barefoot he would never make it to the cave. It had to be the Hole they were looking for. What else could anyone be after on that hillside? He wished Delly would just raise an alarm and scare them off, but it didn't seem to be what he had in mind. Up behind Lillicos' he slipped into the shed and in a moment was back, hefting a long, stout axe handle.

"Look here—" Ray managed in a croaking whisper. He couldn't get the rest out. He knew he ought to stop Delly, ought somehow to raise the alarm himself and bring out Uncle Harry and the cousins, but all he did was jerk at Delly's shirt sleeve in nervous protest. Whatever was going on, it had been trying to play itself out from the day he had first climbed the long hill into

Twillys' Green: the past pressing into the present; some old defeat seeking to complete itself. And something—Ray was frightened what it might be—was expected of *him*.

The intruders missed the cave entrance, moving past it and up the little left fork of Greenbrier Creek, a steep little gully that dead-ended where the stream poured down from Up Top. Under cover of their mutterings and the stones that rattled down, Delly made for the thicket masking the cave. Ray came after, as quietly as he could. With the cave's entrance so low, it was awkward going, even without the worry about noise, but he obeyed when Delly motioned him in, even though he thought it foolish. From inside they might be able to keep intruders away from the Hole, but they couldn't raise the Hollow if they wanted help.

Delly backed in after Ray, pulling something that he left wedged in the opening. "Bush," he explained shortly. "Hope they didn't hear." He caught at Ray's hand as he pulled the flashlight from his pocket. "Not yet. That rock heap against the wall? If we shift some over here so's it blocks the hole, then we c'n have the light."

After a bit of awkward groping and some hurried work, it was done, and Ray switched his light on. Delly found one of the carbide lamps and, sheltering it behind a rock back in the corner that was too large to shift, lit it. "Might as well save them batteries," he said, lighting the lamp. But it burned almost too low to see by.

Ray watched the blocked entrance uneasily. "What if they find the hole anyhow?"

"So long as it's dark we got a chance they won't. But they'll be out there buzzing 'round like wasps that smell honey. They can't be at it all night, though. When it gets a little light they got to be careful if they want to make it out of the Hollow with their hides on."

As Delly leaned down to listen by the new rock pile, Ray thought he heard something behind him—a noise down in the mine. Crossing to the crevice he stood listening. Nothing. The flashlight's narrow beam was drowned in the darkness below. Directing it to the sandy floor at his feet, he moved in and down, listening at every step. At the bottom he reached out for the rail that fenced off the drop in floor level along the right-hand wall, but it was not there. As he swung the light across and down, picking out its splintered pieces on the rubble below, the air behind him sang, and a white light flamed behind his eyes.

Sound, like the sea in a conch shell, foamed in his ears. He struggled to call out to Delly, but the cry fell with him.

Shouts and the clang of metal against stone woke him. As the roaring in his ears ebbed, he made out the sound of duller blows and labored breathing. His head hurt fiercely. His eyes opened and then winced shut in pain at the light. What he thought he saw in that split second chilled him. The dark reaches of the mine were gone, and the rubble-filled chasm running along the wall. The stone serpent on the gleaming wall was no longer half plastered over, but hooped, and whole.

O Serpent Katóa who holds up the earth,
Bestir to grant me power
For I shall fill your maw
With sweet destruction . . .

Tekla stood where the chasm should have been, chanting, arms upraised, to the stone image of the power below. There was no mistaking the place, but there was no mine, only a narrow space five, perhaps six, feet wide. It appeared to be the original crevasse opening downward from the cave, slicing like a wound into the hill. The rubble-filled trough that had run along the black basalt wall was gone too, filled smooth.

The men—Kon and the four others who were in that narrow place—exchanged fearful glances. One spied Ray watching and hauled him to his feet. "You wake in time for your reward," he said with a nervous wolfish grin.

Torches had been set into wall brackets fashioned of some metal crusted with age, and as Tekla swayed in her trance, their light seemed to dim and the still air grew too thick almost to breathe. The weight of that darkness pressed upon the others, but Tekla suddenly knelt and, brushing with her hands like frantic birds' wings, swept away the sand from a patch of floor. In a moment she found what she searched for and brushed frantically again until she had uncovered a long seam marking the edge of a deeper fissure that once had cut down toward the mountain's roots. A great crack had been filled and then surfaced with stone paving so cunningly wrought that the stones interlocked like the pieces of a giant's puzzle.

"A seal! One of them must be a seal." The woman's whisper was hoarse. She ran her hands across the paving stones. Those immediately below and in front of the section of wall, where the serpent's head was, were set in a series of concentric rings. "*Ai, kuutelá!* There are signs here, but they burn." She snatched her hand away and pushed to her feet, swaying. "Bring me Ruan!"

Rough hands thrust Ray forward, and the woman's fingers fastened into his shoulder like talons. "Read!"

"I *can't*," he said. The fingers tightened. "It's *true*. I've never seen letters like that in my life before." And it was true. The shapes circling the stone seal were free, as fluid as flame; not the patterned squares and circles of the Gare books.

Tekla thrust him away and snatched a sword from one of the men. Kneeling, she scrabbled with it at the rim of one of the smaller stones. The torchlight was almost smothered. Ray's ears pounded as thunderously as his heart. In a moment Tekla threw the sword away in disgust. "Pah, it is as soft as butter." Her hand went to the hilt of the longsword hanging at her side.

"These folk have harder metal—they must have tools. Kon! Send one of these gaping fools to search."

"You must not break the seals!"

Above, wrapped in shadow at the top of the sloping passage, a man stood, sword in hand. He was all in shadow, but the silver-pale eyes blazed in the torchlight. He moved slowly, as if it were a great effort.

"What, not finished?" Tekla mastered her fear. "Come then—'Elzevir' did they call you? Read me out this riddle." She pointed to the stones.

"Not a riddle. A doom." Holding Tekla's eyes with his own, he recited softly.

> *Despair be his who breaks the seal,*
> *Slavery his who unbinds the bonds.*
> *For then teeth shall rend the hills*
> *And a shadow cover your lands.*

As the voice died away into the frightened silence, Ray saw the man's hand slip down the wall. He fell heavily, his long length stretched down the stony slope.

Ray felt a tearing at his heart, and in a dreamlike daze saw the boy Ruan pull free of him. Half-shaven head, embroidered tunic, hands, feet, all—ripping away from him, erasing him like an image beneath the plastic sheet on a child's magic blackboard. *"My lord,"* he cried. *"I did not know! I meant no harm. I meant only to buy my freedom. Oh, please my lord, do not be dead."*

Then that other boy drew his hands away, for Elzevir's blue tunic was stained as red as wine.

A Decision

Delly was all right. Or, at any rate, all in one piece. There was an angry puffiness around his right eye, and he dabbed at a cut on one cheekbone with a crumpled bandanna.

Ray turned away from the glare of lantern light and squatted down on the creek bank to cup his hands in the chilly water and splash his face. He would have liked to stick his head right under but was still so dizzy that he knew he'd topple in and have to be fished out like a drowned puppy.

Roney chuckled. "Boy, it's a good thing you got a hard head."

Uncle Dream grinned. "He does have a way of gettin' it cracked." Stooping, he rinsed a frayed red bandanna in the water, wrung it out, and laid it across the back of Ray's neck. "There you go."

"What're we gonter do about this one?" drawled Uncle Harry.

Ray turned his head gingerly, holding the rag to his neck. At the edge of the kerosene lantern's light he saw the stretched-out figure of a man dressed in levis and a dark navy pullover. He was wearing gloves and, grotesquely, a dark nylon stocking over his head that was now pulled up to his forehead.

As they stood regarding him thoughtfully, the man stirred and groaned.

"Who is he?" Ray said.

"One of them Hendrickses from over the other side of the Knob." Uncle Harry guessed. "I ain't sure, but them buck teeth look Hendricks to me."

"Well . . ." Uncle Dream rubbed his stubble of beard and looked perplexed. "What *are* we goin' to do with him? They didn't steal nothing, but sure as little green apples they weren't up to no good. You sure you didn't know any of the other three, Delly?"

"No . . . I don't know." Delly frowned. "There *was* something. Ray, he yelled, and then the one that had got in ahead of us come charging up. But it was all so fast. . . ."

"Don't you worry, boy," Adney said kindly. "It'll come to you."

Ray watched Delly in wonder. He might be a shy,

uncertain young man whose hands were shaking badly, but he had routed four men with little more than a scratch and a promising black eye to show for it. The noise of his scuffle with Ray's assailant had apparently drawn the other three to the cave's entrance, which they promptly cleared; but in that dark, cramped space, Delly's axe handle had a distinct advantage over hunting knives.

"Tell you what," Roney said. "Dream says him and Ad got to go down to Taggert tomorrow to see some lawyer-feller. How about, if I get the truck goin', we take our night-caller here down with us and give him to the sheriff?"

"Good enough," Uncle Harry said. "Me and Delly'll shut him up in our old corncrib for the night. It's stout enough to hold him if somebody's got a padlock."

As the others moved off, Uncle Dream felt the back of Ray's head with gentle fingers and then helped him up with a hand under his elbow. "That's goin' to be a real turkey egg," he said. "Best you don't let on to Star how you come by it. Less she has to fret about right now, the better."

Ray nodded. Even nodding hurt.

Wednesday morning dawned bright and beautiful, but Ray could not bear to look at it.

Rainelle yelled up the ladder-well at seven. "You comin'?"

"No." Ray groaned into his pillow.

"No skin off *my* nose," Rainelle said a little huffily,

poking her head up into the loft. "I got music class to-day, so I guess I'll go along anyhow." After a pause she offered, "Daddy and them are goin' in to Taggert. You hear 'bout that man they caught? He's gone. Busted out of Uncle Harry's corncrib and took off." When there was no answer she shrugged, and slipped down and away.

By mid-morning, with the help of a cup of strong black coffee and a poultice sent down by Aunt Mavee, Ray felt considerably better—a good thing, because the poultice, unwrapped, smelt dreadful. Aunt Star, catching a whiff of it, had grimaced as she showed him how to hold the mess against his scalp. It set up a tingle right away.

"Oh, goodness knows what's in it," Aunt Star said to his question. She leaned forward over the sink, her eyes closed. There was a fine film of sweat on her forehead, but she looked pale, more chilled than warm.

"You all right?"

"I will be." She laughed, a little shakily. "I will be soon as you take that thing and doctor yourself outside."

Ray went out onto the back stoop and, wrapping the big moonseed leaves back around the gummy poultice, slung it far up the hillside. He rinsed the rest off his hair as best he could. His head still throbbed, but the pain wasn't as bad as the cure.

Inside, Aunt Star was sitting in the rocker. "Jody's down to Opal's," she said, "playing with Sweet William. But Mary-Mary's just out front, digging in the yard. I wonder could you walk her across to Erla's? She's real good with Erla."

Ray was alarmed. "Sure. But hadn't I ought to fetch Cousin Erla over here instead?"

Aunt Star laughed. "No, no, honey. I'm only the least little bit tired. The baby's weeks off. It's just I didn't get one wink of sleep last night."

"O.K. . . . if you're sure."

From Lillicos' Ray drifted down to Matticks' for a look at the corncrib. It was stoutly built of two-by-fours, shingle-roofed, and covered with heavy half-inch mesh wire hardware cloth. There were bulges in the wire cloth where the man had apparently thrown his weight against it, but the heavy staple-nails had held, as had the chain and padlock fastening the door. He had got out, in the end, through the floor. For several feet around, the ground was torn up from the digging that had scooped a passage beneath the heavy foundation-frame, and the soft dirt was full of tracks. Not just the man's; but animal tracks as well. Many were small, but some were larger than a dog's. Ray thought uncomfortably of Delly's tale of the gatherings up in the Miggen. But surely it was impossible that varmints should ally themselves with men . . .

Once back across the creek, Ray found Aunt Star curled up on the old sofa, sound asleep, so he tiptoed out again and sat in Uncle Dream's spot on the front porch. He wanted to go Up Top to have another look for Lillico's translation, but he was afraid to leave Aunt Star alone. Without the book Lillico had Englished, there seemed little hope of understanding why the deep past should still lurk so close under the surface of Twillys'

Green. More to the point, why did *he* feel it more than, say, Rainelle or Aunt Star, or even Uncle Penn? Whenever he let his guard down, there it was: a world, right here, of strange, wild people. Ray felt the goose egg on the back of his head carefully and winced.

O.K. So the Watchers, for whatever reason, were here to guard Tûl Isgrun-under-the-hill. They had endured and been faithful even after they'd pretty well forgotten what they had been set to watch over. There must have been a time in the Green, when folk still lived Up Top, when everybody knew the old tales and understood the old songs. It was not likely that they would always have been passed down as haphazardly as they had since Lillico's time. The least accident could have wiped the old lore out forever. Even so, in two hundred years it had withered up and mostly blown away.

And Ray himself? It had been—what? Six days? Not quite a week, and yet his universe had shifted underfoot and overhead. It was changed and so was he, and it was not just the sense, so unexpected and so deep, of belonging; for the idea of staying for good still terrified him. But the precious bus ticket left him cold. He hadn't even told Uncle Dream about it. It was as if he had something to do here. Or undo.

Or undo. Was Ruan the key? Ray might have been inside his skin, but it had gone no deeper than that. Still, he could guess a little. Ruan had to be desperate for his freedom to buy it with the betrayal of his own people, and a fool to think it could be bought. Once people like Tekla had what they wanted, they figured "Why pay for it?" Maybe Arbie Moar was one of them. Ray stirred uncomfortably. He had felt an instinctive distrust of the man from the start, but he had pocketed that distrust along with Arbie's money.

It was strange to think of it, but Ray supposed that he and Ruan might share blood ties too, even though it must run pretty thin after all those years, however many. Lillico's journal suggested that the Latin "boke" was about six hundred years old in 1730, and if the "A.D. CCCXXX" he had seen after the heading *Túl Isgrun* meant the year 330, as his fuzzy recollection from math class suggested, Ruan must have lived a good thousand years or more before Christopher Columbus. It was an eerie thought.

Eerie but exciting.

The present troubles were less so. Eerie, perhaps, but disquietingly so. Ray's thoughts kept drifting back to Arbie Moar: his obsession with the stone serpent, the Hoop Hollow rituals, the prowlers, and Twillys' Green. But what sort of threat to anyone was a hick storekeeper? The idea of Arbie Moar ravaging the countryside, "rending the hills" with his teeth was laughable. But what about Arbie Moar and company sneaking in with nylon stockings over their heads? For, disguise or no, Delly was convinced that Arbie was the stocky man who had been before them down in the mine.

However much he picked at it, the puzzle remained a puzzle.

For lunch, Ray heated up some leftover beans and wondered what people in Twillys' Green did in the heat of midsummer without refrigerators. The beans smelled sweet enough after a night in the pot, but, with the whitish skin of fat over the top, they looked like something that ought to be buried. He doctored them up with salt and pepper, and Aunt Star ate a plateful even if she did wrinkle up her nose at the unaccustomed snap of flavor.

By mid-afternoon Ray had made up his mind about the bus ticket. Wrapping it in a brief note—how could you really explain?—he sealed it in one of Aura Lee's ready-addressed envelopes. "If you're still feeling better, maybe I ought to go down to meet the school bus," he said to Aunt Star. "Delly went down to Taggert with Uncle Dream and them, so there's nobody to keep an eye on the kids."

Afterward, on the way down the hill, Ray felt a little foolish. Old Delly had a need to protect everybody from heaven-knows-what, but about all the girls were in danger of was a bit of teasing from that road crew. Why couldn't he simply have said that he meant to go mail a letter? But perhaps he would have come to meet the bus, letter or no. Rainelle was a good kid, but how could she look out for the little ones—or herself—when she was almost as nearsighted as a mole?

To Ray's relief, Arbie Moar was nowhere in evidence at the Corners. Maclehose the mailman had been and gone, but Ray did not much care. The letter could go out tomorrow as well as today. When the bus pulled in, he collected Rainelle and June Ann, Dawn and Bob-White, and herded them across and up the road in spite of protests.

"No, you're *not* going in," he said firmly. "You got any money? I didn't think so. Why go in and moon over a lot of junk you can't buy? Here, I got us some lemon drops." He brought out a small package and shared it around, two apiece.

Rainelle peered at him curiously. "What's the matter? You sound like a broody old hen."

"Nothing." Ray pretended to be absorbed in sharing out the lemon drops. But he was relieved when they had passed the Sour Creek and Horse Hollow turnoffs without meeting road equipment and strangers. They had got as far as Straight-Up Creek when Roney's pickup overtook them.

"Climb aboard," Roney yelled, as the truck slowed down.

Uncle Harry Mattick was in the cab beside Roney. The rest, sitting in the back, scrambled up to give the kids a hand as Roney shifted into low but did not stop. "I ain't about to push my luck," he yelled. "This old thing c'n lay down an' die when she gets to the top, but she ain't gonter stop now!"

Ray boosted the younger children up to the waiting hands. After Rainelle was safely in, he got a foothold on the rear bumper and rolled neatly over the tailgate, breathless with laughter.

But Uncle Dream and Adney and Delly were grim.

"I got my squirrel gun," Adney was saying, "and Pa's old Iver Johnson single-barrel. Uncle Roy, he's O.K., but Uncle Penn, he ain't got a thing Up Top but that little old Sharps. Even if there's caps for it, which I doubt, it's more like to blow up in his face than shoot."

Uncle Dream shook his head unhappily. "I got that thirty-ought-six, but I never thought to point it at anything more'n game."

"How about you, Delly?" Adney asked gently.

Delly flinched, startled, and brought himself back from somewhere far away. "There's Frank's old shotgun," he said slowly. "But I won't lift it against no man. There's got to be other ways."

Uncle Dream laid a hand on Delly's knee. "You keep to that, boy. I ain't so sure but you may be right, only . . ."

Bob-White was open-mouthed with bewildered excitement. The girls were just plain bewildered.

"What's happened?" Ray asked warily.

Cousin Adney snorted. "The Green's done for. Up Top, th' Hollow, ever'thing. Without so much as a by-your-leave." His voice was tight and his eyes hard. "You tell 'em, Dream. I cain't."

The Will

The Matticks, Uncle Harry and Delly, had gone in to
Taggert just to be going. With the trespasser fled, there
was not much point in filing a complaint. For every
Hendricks of the right size and shape, there would be
two other Hendrickses to swear he had not been outside
the front door. Instead, Harry meant to have a beer with
Roney and see what was new in town. Roney had not
seen Taggert since the day over twenty years before
when he came home from the Korean war. Uncle Harry
had been up two years ago when he and Aunt Luce
had gone to meet Delly, coming home the first time from

the VA Hospital in Beckley, but that had been just in-and-out.

Roney parked in front of the courthouse. The small building housing the lawyers' offices was just next door. He and the Matticks decided to go in with Dream and Adney, and afterward they'd all have a look-see around town together.

Mr. Pilwell, the lawyer, was a little startled when his secretary ushered in five Relatives of the Deceased instead of two, but he recovered nicely, shaking hands all around, and excusing himself to help the secretary bring in three folding wooden chairs.

"There now!" He settled back into his swivel chair. "I feel we ought to be having a full-fledged Reading of the Will, not just these minor bequests, with so many of Mrs. Tullo's kin on hand. I fear I've brought you all a very long way on a very small matter. May I offer you a cup of coffee?"

"No, thanks. Fact is," said Cousin Adney, sitting straight and formal, "we come out of pure curiosity. They ain't a thing Ma owned she hadn't already give away. What she went and made a will for beats me."

"And *how* she did it," Dream put in. "Aunt Neva never got further'n Moars' Corners but twice in her life, and that was when Ad took her to the doc's."

"Y'see," Adney explained earnestly, "her and Pa deeded their land up in the Green—and the house— over to me'n Opal when we got married, so as to save botherin' later. She—"

Mr. Pilwell held up a hand. "Yes, yes, I'm sure all

that's true, but that would have been your father's property, wouldn't it?"

Adney shrugged. "Mebbe on paper."

"Exactly." The lawyer pulled his glasses down from his forehead and peered at the paper on the desk before him. "However, the will which was probated last week dealt with property that Mrs. Tullo held in her own right. Now, I did not draw up the will. It was witnessed and sworn to before a justice of the peace on"—he turned back to the top page—"on the twenty-eighth of last December. When the court found you'd not been notified about the will and probate, they asked that I get in touch with you at once. Let's see now . . ." He ran a finger down the margin. "Yes, here it is."

He looked up briefly, to smile. "It's really rather touching. Mrs. Tullo deposes here that all the things she is leaving, she has come by rightly. She says here, 'To my son Adney I give the gold coins my Daddy gave me the day I was wed, and Adney is to see to the following: for Adney's Opal, the recipe for Brenegar Cake she's always wanted; to my dear granddaughter Sue Ellen I leave my engagement ring; and to my nephew Durham, who is so like his granddaddy, the old silver repeater watch his granddaddy always carried. I should have given it to him long ago, but it was the only thing I had that was my Daddy's own. Last of all, Adney is to give to young Bonethy Yanto, my first cousin twice-removed, the old silver case I had from Grandma Adlonna Mattick, of whom she is the spit and image just as all said I was as a girl. It's to go to her daughter if she has one, and if not, to the youngster who's most like her. These things are all wrapped up careful and stowed in a box under the floorboard beside my bed."

Mr. Pilwell folded the paper tidily. "And that's about it."

"I'll be a twelve-toed hop-toad!" Adney grinned and shook his head. "I never knew Ma had any such things. She never ever wore no engagement ring. Only that thin old wedding band."

"I bet she had a ring from that Harvey Potter," Dream said slowly. "Used to live down at the Corners. Seems I remember Pa saying she was sweet on him. Got hisself kilt in the First World War."

"Well, well." Mr. Pilwell shuffled the papers around on his desk, straightening up the piles. "That does seem to be it, gentlemen. I'm surely glad to've met you all. So long as there's no questions . . ." He looked at his watch. "I'm due over in the magistrate's court in a few minutes. I do thank you gentlemen for coming in."

There was an awkward scraping of chairs, and Mr. Pilwell was shaking hands all around when Delly's soft question brought everyone up short.

"Mr. Pilwell? You said these things of Aunt Neva's were 'minor bequests.' Does that mean there was something else besides? It looks like there's a good bit more on that paper than what you read."

The lawyer's expression of friendly satisfaction wavered. Slowly, as if he were choosing his words with caution, he said, "Yes, there was. But I assumed that you"—he waved his hand to include them all—"that you knew about it. The bequest did not directly involve the family. Surely . . . well, now, I see that you *didn't* know." He paused, then said, "It was that little piece of land Mrs. Tullo left to some church-or-other up your way."

"Land?" Adney asked blankly. "She didn't have no land."

Mr. Pilwell readjusted his spectacles and, folding back the blue cover of the will, scanned the first page. "Yes, here we are: 'My own plot at the north-east corner of Twillys' Green Hollow, I give to Hoop Twofold Church to sell or rent, with the understanding that no outsiders can live on it; only Twillys' Green folk. I do this because the church needs money to get a preacher coming regular again. I have sore missed the good preaching.' "

"I take it," said Lawyer Pilwell, looking from face to face, "that this church has not been in touch with you?"

Dream was fit to be tied. "That's a lot of hogwash," he said angrily. "That land's mine. It's Clewarek land."

"Oh, dear me. No, Mr. Clewarek. I'm very much afraid that there's been a—er, family misunderstanding here. I *am* sorry. But there's no mistake. The deed has been proven, and everything is quite in order. The title has been transferred to this Hoop Twofold Church—or no, I see by my note here that they've changed the name to 'Hoop Church of the Testifiers to the Power.' Odd. But no matter. Title was transferred last week, and I understand that they have since disposed of it."

"Disposed of it?" Delly stiffened.

Mr. Pilwell took refuge behind his desk and an embarrassed and sympathetic manner. "So I gathered. I haven't heard any more than that. It's most unfortunate. The church elders seem to have gone contrary to the spirit of the will in not contacting you first, but they did not go against the letter. Mrs. Tullo did not stipulate that the *whole* use of the property be restricted to you folks up in Twillys' Green, only the right of domicile— er, the right of living on it. She may not have understood the importance of the difference . . ." He trailed off, spreading his hands helplessly.

Adney looked wildly at Roney and Roney at Dream.

"I think," said Uncle Harry grimly, heading for the door, "we'll just pay us a visit to Judge Dishart."

Judge Dishart, to his secretary's surprise, had the five grim hillmen shown in immediately. "Harry Mattick?" had come the surprised rumble from the inner office. "Old Harry and I were in the same outfit in the Pacific back in '45. Show them in!"

Judge Dishart, a big, burly man with a red face, gray hair, and remarkable thick black eyebrows, r'ared up behind his desk. "Harry Mattick, you old sonofagun! What in blazes brings you down out of the hills?"

The judge shook hands around and asked after Uncle Penn and several of the aunts by name. He called Delly "Delano," and said how sorry he'd been to hear about young Frank. When Uncle Harry managed at last to get a word in about Aunt Neva's will, the judge sent his secretary scurrying down to the County Recorder's office and got on the telephone himself to have someone run down the justice of the peace who had witnessed the will.

The J.P., it turned out, had been invited to a Saturday supper at Brother Harkis's in Hoop Hollow and to the prayer meeting that followed. No, it had been an ordinary little service, nice enough. Old Mrs. Tullo was there. After service they'd talked over the will and the old lady had signed it quite willingly. Mrs. Moar and a friend of hers had witnessed it. Couldn't be more legal. The J.P. had given her a ride as far as the turnaround at the end of the county road.

The secretary returned from the Recorder's Office with a report that the plot in question had originally been transferred from Osmel Clewarek to his daughter, Divendly Viana Clewarek, on the twentieth of August, 1920.

"Grandpa Clewarek died the same year," Dream said.

Adney nodded. "Pa tried to court Ma about then, but she'd have none of it. Took him five years to change her mind."

"Maybe," put in Judge Dishart, raising his remarkable eyebrows, "your granddaddy was afraid she meant it, and might be left high and dry with no one to provide for her. He made sure she would at least have a bit of land."

"She sure never let on it was hers," Dream said uneasily. "My daddy thought it was his. Why, I've had a patch of corn in down there ever' summer since Star'n me was married."

The judge sat back, drumming his fingers on the desk.

"Obviously, the thing to do is to find out who bought it from Hoop Church. It can't have much value to an outsider. Likely you can get it back for a few more dollars than they put out. I know there's coal up there, but nobody in his right mind is going to run a road up that mountain for two-three hundred tons of coal."

He picked up the telephone and punched the button for the outer office. "Shirley, did Bob Stringer's office say who the new owner of record was on that old Clewarek property? Oh. Yes, I see." The bluff, hearty manner was suddenly subdued. "You got the number there? Thanks." Hanging up, he scribbled on his notepad and frowned at it thoughtfully. "The Deep Run Coal Company."

Uncle Harry stared. "Why the Sam Hill would a big outfit like that want a little two-bit patch like Neva's?"

Judge Dishart picked up the phone again, almost reluctantly. Put through to Deep Run's main office in Williamson, he asked a few questions, made some notes, and nodded, looking more solemn with every nod. When Delly slipped from the room, he did not notice, and when he hung up, he evaded Uncle Harry's eye.

"I'm afraid you folks aren't going to like this, but it can't come as a complete surprise. Not with the country needing coal the way it does. Deep Run says their graders are moving out of Horse Hollow tomorrow and up your way. They mean to have the grading done by the weekend, and bring the bulldozers and coal drills in on Monday to start driving a main entry."

"For that little dab of coal?" Adney was incredulous.

The judge cleared his throat. "Well, no. They're going after the whole mountain. Seems you've got some broad uplands up there—not like these hog-back ridges we've got everywhere else in the county. The fellow I talked to just now says there's got to be a good thick seam up there, and now that they have these surface rights at the foot of your hollow, they can just go straight in. It's a real windfall for the county. A lot of jobs. Lots of money . . ." His voice trailed off into the horrified silence.

Dream could hardly believe his ears. "You tellin' us they think they got the mineral rights to the Hollow and Up Top? Well, they *don't.* There's not one acre, not a square yard of coal rights been sold out from under our land. That coal's ours. When them slickers come around in the 'eighties buyin' up rights, Uncle Penn's granddaddy told 'em just what they could do with their half-dollar-an-acre and kicked 'em down the mountain. How do they get off sayin' they can just go in and take it?"

Judge Dishart was distressed. "I hardly think—" he said.

Uncle Harry skewered him with a sharp look. "Easy enough to call 'em back and check it out."

The judge drew a nervous hand through his hair. "Look here, Harry. You're an old friend and all that, and believe me, I value that friendship, but—well, you know how it is. Being a public servant, I really can't take sides in these things." He frowned heavily, his smoothness recovered. "If there is any fraud—and I don't for a moment say there is—but if there were, it would be most improper for me to've advised you. If the case came up before me in court and the company thought I'd been poking around in their affairs beforehand, well, it just wouldn't be proper. What you need to do"—he scrawled something on a fresh sheet of his notepad—"is to see Erwin Smalley. He's with Cooper, Pilwell and Smalley. Best attorneys in town." He tore off the sheet and handed it to Uncle Harry with unmistakable finality.

The cousins, bewildered and angry, stood silent as Harry accepted the paper, folded it carefully, and stuck it in his shirt pocket. All Uncle Harry said was, "If you're sure that's how you feel, Will." He led the way out.

They were in the wide front hall, arguing in fierce undertones when Delly came out of the County Recorder's Office. Making a sign to his father, he headed out to the truck parked at the curb in front. When the others had joined him on the sidewalk, he explained.

"The minute I heard 'Deep Run Coal' I knew they weren't in it for the few tons they'd get out of Aunt Neva's two acres. They're too big. So I went to see this guy in the Recorder's Office I was in school with. He looked in the old files and says they got a copy in there of a deed to all our coal rights. Even Up Top. It's dated 1885 and only signed with an X, but there's a notary's signature sayin' the X belongs to Denoon Yanto."

"Uncle *Denoon*?" Roney snorted. "Hell, he was a half-wit! Besides, no one body could sign away all them rights. Not even one parcel of 'em. Back then, the whole shebang belonged to everybody together. It hadn't been divvied up at all."

"Just a minute, now." Uncle Harry held up both hands. "Do you mean that coal company's just been sittin' on that piece of paper for near a hundred years, just bidin' time till they got a toehold in the Hollow so's they could get at it?"

"No," Delly said. "The deed's made out to a—a Kennington Iron Company. They must've folded, because it was transferred twice again before Deep Run got aholt of it three years ago."

"Who the Sam Hill *is* this Deep Run Coal Company?" Dream asked plaintively. "A steel company, or just some big cheese up in Williamson?"

Delly's mouth tightened. "Kenny run that down too. Seems it used to be just a broke-down old truck mine over in Mingo County until something called JM Properties bought it up five or six years ago. They own Kentinnia Downs, the race track, and the Speedway in at Willocks, and some kind of big new shopping center over to Mozart. Any good thing they can lay their hands on, I guess."

"Dammit, boy, stop pussyfootin'." Uncle Harry glared. "Who's this 'J.M.'?"

Delly drew a deep breath. "Kenny, he says it must stand for 'Jessica Moar.' It's all in her name. Old Arbie, he's president and chairman of the board."

The Barriers

"You know what else?" Delly rested a moment over the crosscut saw he and Adney were using to dismember another fallen tree above the hill road. "That lawyer, Pilwell? Him and his partners are Arbie Moar's lawyers too. They had us comin' and goin'."

"Slick as hog fat," Adney muttered. He started sawing again with such vigor that Delly, at the other end of the blade, could only hang on to his handle, laughing. It was the first time anybody had so much as smiled since the morning's trip into Taggert.

"Ad," he panted, "slow down. The way you're goin'

194

at this poor tree, you'd think it was Arbie Moar himself."
The tree, an old giant brought down by the wind and
heavy wet snow and its own weakened roots, had already produced ten huge eight-foot lengths to be snaked
down the slope and tipped over onto the road. There,
they were held in place by boulders levered out of the
overhanging bank.

Merle and Ray, sweaty from helping trim the branches
from the crowns of several trees, had been put to work
carrying stones and rolling boulders to wedge beneath
and against the downhill bottom logs. No one boulder,
however large, was a sure block to the weight piling up
behind it. When the first heavy barricade was breast-
high across the narrow washboard road—from the hill's
steep shoulder to the rim where the slope fell away into
the Greenbrier's gully—the men shouldered their tools
and moved a hundred yards uphill to do the same again.
And the closer it got to suppertime, the more determinedly they worked.

No one said much. It seemed to Ray that every one
of them, working so doggedly, soaked with sweat, knew
that their heaps of sticks and stones were futile. But it
was all they could think to do. Like their forebears, they
were ready to do battle with greed and treachery, but
this time the outside world had the stronger weapons.
They might get their battle. Might even win it, here on
their own ground. But they would get so tired and
tangled in the law that they would lose the larger war.

"Look," Ray said to Delly, who had paused to catch
his breath, "there's got to be other lawyers. Isn't there

somebody can swear the old man who signed the paper was soft in the head?"

"Old Denoon?" Roney, lugging a heavy boulder, slipped and almost lost his balance. "He was daft as a criggelly. They say oncet he greased up all his ma's hens because he heard her say there wasn't nothing she liked better'n buttery chicken. Made such a stink of rancid feathers the poor old lady had to give every one of them birds a bath, and to top it all off, two of the dumb clucks drowned."

"Uncle Denoon was the dumb cluck," Adney observed sourly. "I'll bet Uncle Roy could tell a tale or two on the old boy."

"More'n two," Uncle Roy Tullo wheezed. "But I ain't got the puff just now."

Delly motioned to Ray to take the small end of a roughly-trimmed log and bent to heft the other himself. "M' friend down in Taggert says the lawyers there that *ain't* tied in to some coal company or other ain't worth the hire. The only one up in Willocks is old Verl Putz, and he's kin of Jessie Moar's daddy."

Ray let his end down with a *thunk!* where Delly showed him. "Then they're bound to get in here sooner or later."

Uncle Dream appeared beside them. "Later's better'n sooner. Mebbe with a little time we'll think of somethin'."

"Best we're goin' to get is a good fight," Roney said with flat belligerence.

Delly had the look of someone who saw the grim future fall like a sharp shadow across his path. "We got to keep the road graders out, or we'll have miners in the coal seam by Tuesday. After last night, Arbie Moar's got to know where the old shrine is. Tûl Isgrun. It won't take him any time atall to poke an entrance into that hill and head back toward the Hole."

It was the first time he had said it right out in front of everybody. Tûl Isgrun. In the startled silence the words echoed like a threat out of the deeps of childhood. Even Cousin Roney, spoiling for a fight, looked shaken.

"I forgot about that. It's been so long, I forgot. But looky here—all that's just fairy tales, just nonsense they told us when we was bitty kids. Uncle Penn's daddy, he was full of that kind of stuff."

Uncle Dream leaned on his axe. "I dunno. There's a queer feelin' down in that Hole. I recollect Grandma tellin' about when our daddies helped blast the opening at the back of the cave wide enough to let 'em through more easy. Pa, he wouldn't talk about it, but she said Uncle Penn's daddy was prophesying doom and singin' one of them old gibberish poems at 'em." Frowning, he recited haltingly,

> Don't spare him that breaks the sills.
> Enslaved be he that frees th' bonds,
> For teeth shall run th' hills,
> And a shadow cover thy hand.

"I've heard that one," Roney said. "Bunch of nonsense."

"Still, it had them all spooked, didn't it, Uncle Roy?" Adney put in.

"Surely did." The old man shook his head in remembered wonder. "When th' dust cleared an' we went along in, why, th' air was so still an' heavy y' could hear th' blood rushin' round inside y': poundin' in an' rushin' back. Y' couldn't breathe for bein' afeard. I never did understand it. Folks'd been slippin' in an' out of that crack after coal a hundred year or more, an' there'd never been th' like of that. It was a couple weeks afore we got nerved up t' go back."

Roney snorted. "All on account of believin' old pooky tales."

"*What* pooky stories? *I* never heard no stories," Merle complained.

His father shrugged. " 'Watchers.' Wasn't that it, Uncle Roy? Our first-folk was called 'Watchers'?"

Old Uncle Roy Tullo threw his head back and sang in a quavery voice, jiggling a little to the nursery-rhyme tune.

> *Tûl Isgrun was busted down—*
> *Th' canny ones sung fer joy.*
> *But one or two they lasted through*
> *Till help come from th' moon.*
>
> *Eight hundred year they stuck it out,*
> *A-watchin' from Up Top.*
> *An' then th' Tooley tiptoed back,*
> *A-sniffin' out his Hole.*
>
> *He tho't t'was safe and they was gone,*
> *But they was Watchers true.*
> *He went to sleep b'neath a rock,*
> *An' waked to find him under lock.*

Uncle Harry frowned. "I never heard *that* one."

"Well, it ain't nonsense," Delly said. He smiled briefly. "Except maybe for the 'tiptoe' bit. Cousin Dream hasn't said, but he and Ray found something down the Hole: a kind of marker, like, for the old shrine that had been plastered over. Ray says it's a carved stone snake hooped up so real it looks like rolling away. Then Arbie Moar got his hands on a bit of it—never mind how— and it got to pulling at him to come up and get it loose, like it got somebody to loose it once before, breakin' the old seals. How they ever got it shut up again, I don't know, but they did. That's how I read it, anyhow. Now, Arbie Moar, he won't rest him till Tûl Isgrun is busted open again and he's sucked the marrow out of these hills."

The uncles had listened in a leery silence, but Ray knew that Delly was right. Arbie Moar had known that the shrine—or *some*thing—was there long before they did. He may have sensed it when he first came into the hills, felt it whispering at him, sucking at the marrow of his own bones. He had married Jessie, bought out the Crossroads store, and like a spider sat and spun his webs. In time, as the shape of what he sought grew clearer, the circle of his greed grew wider. Poor old Hoop Church. As Arbie was drawn deeper, he drew them after him, playing on their interest in old mountain practices and then easing them right on past into something horribly alien. There wasn't much to choose between Arbie Moar and a sackful of copperheads.

Merle was doggedly skeptical. "O.K., but what's that all *mean*?" Behind him, Roney nodded, but the rest had listened to Delly gravely, for the first time seeing in him something of what Ray had seen—the shadow of a taller man, silver-eyed and sure.

"It means," Delly said, "that the more he gets, the more he wants. Uncle Roy's 'Tooley' is like a worm in his heart. What matters is the *getting*. Look, if there *is* coal all the way back under Up Top, there's ways of taking it out from under without harming men nor trees. They could tunnel in from the south side of Moon if they gave a hoot; but no, they'll leave that side t' clean out with augurs after they've hollowed the hill. The Gare'll tumble down and the waters be drained off. And when old Arbie's done with us, he'll be bigger and hungrier still. *That's* what wants loose from Tûl Is-grun—that bottomless hunger—and Arbie's just a start."

"Hi up there!"

The call came thinly from below the lowest barricade. "Hey, *some*body?"

"Sounds like Bon." Merle shook himself like a puppy waking up.

Roney and Delly hurried down to see. They found a flushed and breathless Bonnie leaning against the piled-up rocks and climbed up on the logs to give her a hand over. Bonnie was startled to see everyone standing above, watching so solemnly. Grabbing at Delly's outstretched hand nervously, she jumped down after her father.

Roney was chagrined that he should have been sweating so hard to wall off the Hollow without a thought for Bonnie's being stuck down at the store. He said gruffly, "Pretty late, ain't you, honey? How come you got yourself so steamed up?"

Bonnie flushed darkly under her makeup. "I'd've been sooner," she said, "only I was afraid if Mr. Moar thought I was hurrying off before closing time to tattle, he'd maybe try to stop me. This way he don't know I heard. He was on the phone in his office talking to some judge, saying how he'd heard you was all in the hardware store down in Taggert buying shotgun shells after you come out of the courthouse. He wanted to know what was up."

"Why, the old snake!" Roney muttered. "Sorry, hon. You go on."

Bonnie shrugged. "You'd've thought he was some kind of High Muckety-Muck. He orders this judge to put out a 'straining order and send the sheriff over here with it when the road crews come in tomorrow morning. What's it all about?"

"Well, well," Uncle Harry drawled. "And I'll just bet old Will Dishart knuckled right under. Let's us hope nobody loses his head tomorrow."

"What's *happened*?"

"Uncle Penn's goin' to say 'No guns.' You know he is," Adney offered.

Roney gave him a mulish look. "If he thinks I'm goin' to sit on my behind while they rip up the prettiest green earth I ever seen, he'll have another think coming."

"Won't somebody tell me?" Bonnie wailed.

After supper everyone met by the Matticks' front porch to argue what was best to do. They had lived too long to themselves and had too few dealings with the outside to know. Except for men going off to war and the children off to school, their dealings had for the most part been with the Crossroads store. Arbie Moar *was* the outside; and now that that world's face had changed they were at a loss to know how to meet it.

Delly sat apart, lost in thought, while they wrangled. Ray watched him, disappointed. He did not quite know what he had expected—some wise word to unravel the legal knot? Or a flashing sword to cut it through? But Delly, for all his flashes of strength, was no Elzevir.

In the end, the only thing decided upon was Uncle Penn's suggestion, that a watch be kept through the night at the lower barricade "in case that sneakin' copperhead tries to pull a fast one."

At nine Delly had unaccountably disappeared, so it was Merle and Adney who set off for the first stint. At midnight Ray, who hadn't been able to sleep anyway, came down early with Uncle Harry. At four, Uncle Dream and Roney came and sent them back up to their beds. Everyone was up at the crack of dawn, and after an early breakfast all the men, Uncle Penn included, headed down the hill.

Ray thought it a little spooky that no one mentioned Delly's being missing. They were so busy not mentioning it that they might as well have said right out, "Delly's got his up and downs still. Best not count on *him*."

Bonnie and Rainelle followed them down a little later, carrying between them a large enamel coffee pot to set in the coals of the fire that had warmed the night watchers and a sackful of battered tin cups.

For a while the gathering was almost light-hearted. "Y' know, Ad," Dream said, "we clean forgot about diggin' Aunt Neva's goodies up from under your back bedroom floor. At least some of us'll get somethin' out of all this."

A few minutes before eight o'clock they heard the throb of heavy engines far down the valley: a sound that grew steadily closer.

Besieged

First in sight at the wide place down by the old mail-boxes were two blue county cars sporting the sheriff's seal in black and silver on the doors. The first, a station wagon, started up the grade, but the stony ruts were so deep and the center ridge so high that its low-slung muffler scraped bottom noisily. After a moment the wagon gingerly backed down to where the second car waited. The men—three officers and two in street clothes —got out and peered undecidedly up the dark gloom of the steep, tree-shadowed road. Behind them the first road grader pulled up and stopped. The driver did not get down but settled himself against the steering wheel to watch.

Two of the deputies started up the hill. When they saw the high log barricade and the grim men behind it, they slowed a little, but then came on as the sheriff and the others caught up.

"Ain't that old Verl Putz?" Adney indicated the skinny-limbed, pot-bellied man in a dark suit who was taking care to keep well behind the sheriff's considerable bulk.

"Yeah," Roney said. "In the ugly flesh. And that deputy there, the tall one? That's got to be one of the Yunnie boys. Never was a Yunnie didn't have flap ears."

Below, the sheriff, zippered into an olive-green windbreaker which might have served a smaller man for a tent, bellowed up the slope. "One of you men Penn Dreego?"

"Right here." Uncle Penn stepped one log up. "And who might you be? This here's a private road."

"Sorry, Mr. Dreego, but I'm Sheriff Slimman, and I got a court order here says different. Deep Run Coal Company's got right of access up to that plot of land they own."

"That one they *stole*, you mean," the old man snapped back at him. "They tricked a poor old woman into thinkin' she could give it away an' still keep it safe. Young Verl Putz down there, he might know somethin' about that. Was it you wrote that paper out for Miz Tullo, Putz? You're a J.P., ain't you?"

Putz gobbled a little, like a turkey. The sheriff gave

him an uncomfortable look but cleared his throat and tried again. "That ain't my affair. I'm just here to see there's no trouble." Pulling a paper from his inside jacket pocket, he proceeded to read the formally worded order into the sullen silence: ". . . and furthermore, the Court enjoins and commands that said persons shall not hinder, delay, or harass the employees of said company by denying to said employees access to and full use of the road known as Dreegos' Hill Road, to which they are entitled."

The sheriff folded the paper and tucked it away. "That's signed by Judge Dishart for the Third Circuit County Court," he called. "It says straight out you got no call to block this road, so you men set to and start humping them logs over the hill."

No one moved.

"C'mon, now. We know you don't like it. I don't like it much myself. But you ain't doin' yourselves a bit of good this way."

When there was still no answer, he reddened and muttered something to himself. After a moment's hesitation he turned and gave a quiet order to the tallest of the uniformed men. The officer went down to the second car, opened the trunk, and in a moment was back with a gasoline-powered chain saw. He was within ten yards of the barricade when a shotgun blast tore through the branches over his head. Bits of leaves drifted down like confetti.

"What in blazes? Yanto, you like to take my ear off!"

"Just flatten it back some," Roney yelled. "You ought

to know better'n to come up here, Yunnie. Your Horse Hollow kin don't have cause to love Arbie Moar any more'n Twillys' Green."

"Arbie Moar? What's he got to do with it?" The deputy looked genuinely puzzled.

"Sheriff there didn't tell you? Why, old Arbie, he *is* Deep Run Coal Company."

"Is he now?" said the deputy softly. "Well now, that's real interesting. I'll remember that. But it don't make a bit of difference right now. You got to move or we got to take you in. Hit's our job."

"I hope you get paid real good for it," Uncle Harry drawled.

Yunnie went back down for a word with the sheriff and the others. Verl Putz was doing a lot of finger-shaking, and the sheriff didn't look any too happy. He looked even less so when a large stake-bed truck pulled up past the parked road graders and came to a stop just below his own car. The fifteen or twenty men crowded in the back were dressed in tan with some sort of shoulder patch and were armed with shotguns.

Uncle Penn turned briefly. "Get them kids out of here."

Uncle Dream nodded. "Bonnie? Merle c'n stay, but you get Rainelle and Ray up behind that next stack of logs, quick. Then up th' hill, one at a time."

Bonnie didn't waste words, but gave Rainelle a shove and pushed Ray along after her. As they ran, the sheriff was calling down to the truck, "Who in blazes you think you are, coming up here tricked out like that?"

A big red-headed man who had ridden in the cab with the driver got out and slammed the door. "Security police, Deep Run Coal Company, sir. We're just here to see they don't give you any trouble."

The sheriff turned ominously purple and growled, "Well, you can just turn around and get the Sam Hill out of here."

There was no answer for a moment, and then the man's smooth, heavy voice said, "Well, now, sir, I'm sorry. We just can't do that."

Up behind the second barricade Bonnie gave Ray a shove, and he went haring uphill after Rainelle.

Bonnie was last up by a good ten minutes. Ray and the aunts and cousins were waiting for her by the bridge beyond the road's crest, Aunt Mavee at their head.

"Well, what is it?" the old lady snapped. "What's happened?"

Bonnie stopped a moment to catch her breath and then said, "Sheriff's took them all in to county jail. There wast just too many of them guards, and they was bent on pickin' a fight. Uncle Penn and the sheriff, they yelled back and forth for a bit, and then the deputies got their guns and come up to that old log pile to talk. I dunno what they said, but two of the deputies stayed right there, and Daddy and Cousin Dream and them went down and clumb in the cars."

Sue Ellen was perplexed. "You mean they arrested ever'body and're still keepin' the road closed?"

"It looked like. But you can bet two of 'em ain't gonna keep it closed for long, badges or no."

"That sheriff's got somethin' in his head, but there's no tellin' what it is," Aunt Mavee said briskly, "so we'd best get to work. Your Uncle Penn's got a sledge hammer Up Top, and we'll need them axes and saws the boys was workin' with yesterday." She raked a sharp eye over the little gathering. "Erla, you and Star'd best take your youngest along Up Top now. Aunt Bessie too. Star ain't in any shape for heavy work, and Erla'll need a hand with the young uns. You too, young man," she said sternly to Sweet William, who clung tearfully to Sue Ellen's knee. "Your mama's got work t' do. I reckon Bob-White and June Ann c'n stay a whiles. They're big enough t' tote rocks."

Star and Erla and old Aunt Bessie Tullo went, herding the little ones ahead of them. Luce Mattick, watching them go, asked worriedly, "Aunt Mavee, what d'you mean us to *do*?"

The old woman snorted. "Only what them overgrown boys with their guns an' barricades ought've done: let th' Hollow take care of itself. First off, we take this here bridge out, and then we build us a dam clean across. The neck ain't so wide here, and oncet we close it, th' pond'll back right up. With a nice little spillway, we c'n tip that water straight down th' road. Them ruts is so deep, it'll make a first-rate creek, an' by tomorrow it ought t' be a first-rate mud-slide."

Barricades were more exciting, Ray thought, feeling envious of Merle, getting carted off to the county jail;

but the old lady was right. If those graders couldn't cope with the road, neither could they bull a route through further up the slope, for the beeches and hemlocks on the hill were the giants of a virgin forest, not downland second-growth to be bowled over by the big machines.

The others were delighted. Faye and Opal exchanged grins, and Bonnie hooted right out loud. Ray saw with surprise that the laughter made her fierce, pointed little face almost beautiful, almost—almost like a far-off echo of the woman who had run like the wind to warn Elzevir.

"Don't just stand there like a row of bumps on a log," snapped Aunt Mavee. "Git them tools!"

At noon the creek was already running thinly in the road. The sounds of heavy machinery at work still droned up through the trees—they had started up in mid-morning. There was no telling what had happened to the deputies. By mid-afternoon, however, the creek running in the road must have been making a shambles of the work below. Shortly after four o'clock the engines stopped entirely.

Aunt Luce kept watch at the dam until eight; then Sue Ellen, and at midnight, Ray. The moon had not yet risen above the hills when Bonnie came down at four, wading quietly through the shallows rather than clamber awkwardly along the slope above. She had just reached Ray in the branches of the squat sugar maple at the west end of the dam when together they saw a shadow flicker among the trees in the ravine below.

"Should we ring the bell?" Aunt Mavee had rooted

out an old brass handbell, and it was hanging from the next branch up.

Bonnie laid a hand on Ray's jacket sleeve. "No . . . wait a minute."

The shadow moved swiftly and surely up through the dark-boled beeches along the face of the slope below. The moon, which had just topped the hills, gave enough light through the still-young foliage to see the movement, but not the mover. It was no stranger. It had to be someone who knew the mountain well to have come so far through the deep night of the hill-forest.

"It's Delly!" Bonnie's thin fingers slipped down to hold Ray's wrist so tightly that he winced. "Where's he *been* so long?"

Just below the dam Delly stopped, bewildered by the unexpected brush-and-rubble dam. Behind it, water spread darkly away, pricked with reflected stars. "Glory be!" he breathed.

Bonnie called softly. "Delly? It's us—me'n Ray. Over in the sugar tree. You c'n get up this way."

Delly made it to the base of the stunted tree and leaned wearily against the trunk. He looked tired and worried, but grinned as he waved his hand at the water. "Whose idea was this?"

"Aunt Mavee's," Bonnie said shortly. "You all right? You *sure* you're all right?" She touched his forearm and then withdrew her hand quickly.

Delly was very quiet for a moment, and then he shrugged. "As well as can be. Where is Aunt Mavee? And the others?"

"Some're Up Top. Aunt Mavee's at our house. She—"

Delly cut her off. "Let's go then. You too, Ray. No need to watch for a bit. Everything's quiet all the way down to the Corners." He turned and was gone. In a moment Bonnie was splashing behind.

The old lady was sleeping upright in Roney's rocker, and flickered awake at the first creak of a step on the front porch. "Who's that?"

"Me, Aunt Mavee." Bonnie moved to the table and reached up to grope for the string hanging from the naked ceiling light.

In the next room mattress springs creaked, and Faye appeared in the doorway, rubbing sleep from her eyes. "You back already, honey?"

"Delly's here." Bonnie drew him in from the porch and Ray came behind.

"Who's at the dam?" Aunt Mavee snapped.

"Nobody," Delly said. "No need, Auntie. There's nobody below but a man on guard over the road machines."

"That's as may be. Still oughter be somebody on watch."

"I'll go down," Faye said. "Now I'm up, I'd just as soon go now as at eight."

"It'll wait a minute," Delly insisted. He pulled up a kitchen chair and sat down astraddle. "I went to Williamson. Walked down to Willocks, and caught a ride along to Maclehose's in Taggert. I told the preacher about the hoo-haw up here, and he was real upset. He wanted to charge right down and see to getting Uncle Penn and them out of jail first thing."

" 'Wanted to'? What's that mean?" Aunt Mavee demanded.

"After a bit he figured old Dishart wouldn't let the sheriff hold them for more'n the one night anyhow." Delly smiled wryly. "He may owe R.B. Moar, but he owes Pa too, and he wouldn't like it to get spread around what he did. Anyhow, Preacher said it was more important to find out how bad things really were, so he drove me up to see this lawyer friend of his in Williamson."

Aunt Mavee sighed. "I take it he wasn't much help."

Delly frowned. "Well, yes and no. He said we might have a chance in court if we could find somebody who wasn't kin who could swear old Denoon hadn't more'n half a marble, or somebody who could prove all the land *was* held in common. But the snag there is that none of the land was proper registered until a county survey in '97—and that was when they laid out boundary lines Up Top according to families."

"Pish!" Aunt Mavee waved an impatient hand. "That's because the county wouldn't let 'em record it as belongin' to ever'body." She gave Delly a sharp look and then snapped, "Put on the coffeepot, Bonnie child. This boy's about t' topple over."

Delly shook his head as if to clear it. "I dunno. Mebbe things'll get straightened around legal-like, but if they carve that road up the mountain and come this way into that coal seam, it'll be too late. Arbie Moar means to get at whatever he thinks is under that hill. All he's got to do is get one of them mining machines pointed in the right direction, and he can cut through to the Hole like he was cuttin' through cheese. Only thing—" He broke off in surprise at seeing his mother coming down from the Yantos' loft, where she'd been sleeping in Bonnie's bed. Catching sight of him, Aunt Luce let out a quiet sigh of relief.

"Only thing we can do is slow 'em down," he continued bleakly, "like with your dam. What I'd *like* to do is blow the whole thing up: the mine, Tûl Isgrun and all."

"Well, why not?" Ray said slowly, watching Bonnie stoke up the stove. "It's coal."

Water and Fire

"Fire in the mine?" Aunt Mavee was disapproving.
"What good's keeping other folk out if we end up blowing up the mountain ourselves?"

"It wouldn't do that." Delly was warming to the idea.
"Or anyhow, not much of it."

Cousin Faye looked from Delly to Bonnie nervously.
"Mebbe not, but it's wasteful. And what's to keep it
from burning till Kingdom Come? Roney, he was in Top
Hole Number 2 when they had that fire in the lower
level. They could pump water down in there, but still it
burned for the better part of a month. How you going
to put out one down in our Hole?"

Delly slumped down, chin on his arms atop the chairback.

"Far as its being wasteful," Aunt Mavee said, "if there was a way t' put it out, I'd not grudge spending a bit of coal to save a lot."

Bonnie closed the damper in the stove flue three-quarters shut and picked up the coffeepot to fill more cups. "Anybody wants it with milk, we got powdered." When she finished pouring, she turned back to the stove and stood fiddling with the flue damper as she listened to the others. The vent in the stove's firebox door was half-open, and through it Ray saw the fire blaze up and damp down. As he looked up, his eyes met Bonnie's.

"Would it work?" he blurted, and then flushed as a startled Aunt Mavee broke off in mid-sentence to demand, "Would what?"

"It's just an idea. The stove—a fire won't burn without air, so if you can shut the air off, it's got to go out sooner or later. *Could* you shut the Hole up? Uncle Dream said it was safe from that methane-gas stuff because there was such a good draught through it. That air's got to go someplace if it comes in through the cave. Could it be stoppered up?"

Aunt Mavee gave an approving nod. "There's two-three natural chimneys come out Up Top back along the line of that queer rock wall down in the Hole. Sometimes it blows through so hard they moan like an organ."

"I know where you mean." Delly's pale eyes were alight again. "They could be blocked easy, and the cave entrance shut up. That coal seam isn't exposed any-

wheres near the Hole, so there's no way a fire could
burn its way out to air. It might mean risking an explo-
sion, but there'd be nobody dangered by it, like the
firefighters in the old Top Hole fire would've been.
It'd do no real harm. Might even snuff the fire right out."

Ray nodded excitedly. "That's how they put out oil
well fires—with explosions. I saw it in a movie on TV."

"And I just bet it'll melt that Tûl Isgrun down into
one big clinker," Bonnie said with soft malice. She
flipped the stove damper open and the fire roared cheer-
fully up the flue.

After Faye went down to watch at the dam, Aunt
Mavee returned Up Top with Luce and Sue Ellen and
as much extra bedding as they could carry. Bonnie stayed
down, ignoring Delly's repeated insistence that he needed
no one but Ray. There was nothing to do but give in
to her.

Though dawn was not far off, it was still dark. Delly
sent Ray and Bonnie off with the flashlight to collect
what kerosene there might be, along with any other fuel.
Taking a lantern himself, he disappeared in the direction
of Roney's shed. By first light they had brought to the
outer cave six half-empty kerosene tins, Roney's emer-
gency supply of gas for the truck, six assorted cans of
bacon grease, a gunny sack stuffed tightly with straw,
and a fat ball of clothesline. The considerable pile of
splintered planking among the rubble in the cave was
enough for a modest bonfire itself, and, in stacking it
near the mine entrance, Ray uncovered a grimy tin box

containing half a dozen paper-wrapped cylinders labelled *ATLAS FARM POWDER—The Safest Explosive.*

"What you got there?" Delly asked. "Man, talk about old! Those must be left from way back when they were clearing trees out of the Hollow. Set it down real careful. You can't trust stuff that old. The powder might be safe as pancake flour, and then again it might go off soon as you look at it cross-eyed. We'll leave them and the fuel oil to take in last."

Bonnie went in first, with the lantern and an armload of the shorter scraps of wood. Delly and Ray followed, heavily laden. They were barely into the sloping passage to the mine when the lantern snuffed out.

"What's wrong?"

"I dunno." Bonnie swung the lantern, and they could hear the slosh of oil. "It's a good half-full. I didn't feel any draught, neither. Where's that flashlight?"

Though there was no draught, the passage did seem unusually damp and cold. Remembering his earlier frights, Ray felt a distinct reluctance to go a step further. Unloading his lumber with a clatter, he tugged the flashlight from his jacket pocket and handed it over. "L-look," he blurted nervously. "*It* put the light out. It's not going to let us do it. It *knows.*"

"I wouldn't be atall surprised," Delly said grimly. "You all right, Bon? Mebbe you and Ray ought to go along Up Top."

"Me?" Bonnie scoffed. "It'll take more'n Uncle Roy's old 'Tooley' to spook me." Nonetheless, when she moved ahead, it was cautiously.

The further in they went, the more alarmingly the cold deepened. The light, as it glanced off the walls, showed a streaming dampness far heavier than Ray remembered. Surely coal so wet would never burn? The dampness grew steadily worse as they approached the stretch of wall where the headless serpent arched over the rubble-filled way to the roots of the mountain. There water lay in pools and dripped from every mine-prop and beam. Delly propped the boards he carried against the nearest pillar and looked around him uneasily. "Looks like the whole of the Miggen's drained down through."

Bonnie, her thin shoes already soaked, stepped across another puddle to dump her wood scraps and set the lantern down in a dry spot. "We better light this again. Flashlight won't last forever. You got any more batteries for it, Ray?"

"Back over at the house." Ray watched Bonnie hold the glass lantern-chimney for Delly, who struck and shielded a match that promptly guttered out, as did the second. The third, cupped carefully in his hand, glowed bluely as it touched the wick, smoldered, and then snuffed out.

"It's like trying to light the fool thing under water," Delly grumbled. "We better go out for another load, and Ray can go along over and get them batteries. I got a feeling if we get caught down here in the dark, they'll likely find us drowned."

The air was already so full of moisture that breathing was difficult. Every breath drawn in that chill humidity was like the touch of a dull, cold knife. Leaving the lantern by the pillar, they ran, Bonnie splashing ahead toward the cave and warmth.

Delly was last out. "Y' know, that water *can't* be from the Miggen," he said worriedly. "Bogs are bogs because they got no dainage. It's not rained in a week, and it's scarce snowed, so where'd it all come from?"

Bonnie, sitting on an upended bucket, took off her shoe to tip the water out and stared. It was dry. "But . . ." she began. Sticking out the other foot, she scowled at it too.

The sole was scarcely damp. Ray shivered, even though the cavern was warm and dry. "I told you. It's this place. It's like the first time I was in. Uncle Dream was gone a couple of minutes, only it seemed forever, and all the time the dark creeping up. There was water then, too. Your mind plays tricks on you in there." Or, he thought to himself, whatever it was in there played them on you. And worse. For hadn't it, disastrously, drawn him back that second time?

Delly said nothing, only gathered up several lengths of timber to load on the old wagon. Ray, at Bonnie's sharp nod, turned and ducked out through the opening. When he returned with the flashlight batteries, the wagon was empty again. Bonnie sat huddled on her bucket and Delly on the ground with his head between his knees. As Ray scrambled in, Delly looked up bleakly and pushed himself erect.

"What's wrong? What happened?"

"Nothing much." Delly was grim. "But whatever's in there sure works at you like a worm in an apple."

Bonnie managed a faint grin. "Anyhow, it's left off the cold and wet."

There were only the fuel tins and a few odds and ends left to go in. The cans they loaded into the wagon along with the larger fragments of the stone serpent, which Ray dragged out from their hiding place. Bonnie stowed the box of blasting charges at the bottom of a bucket and the ball of clothesline on top of it. At Delly's questioning look, she said briskly, "If only we get that lantern lit, I figured we could tie this to it, and then give it a tug from a safe ways away. It's not long enough to reach all the way out here, but I've got some string in my pocket might make it long enough. Them old lanterns tip over pretty easy. That's why so many idiots start fires with 'em." She sounded brisk; but when Delly had taken up the flashlight and the wagon handle and led the way back in, she began to tremble. Whatever she had seen or felt in there had shaken her badly. She motioned nervously to Ray. "You go ahead. I'll be right behind."

Bonnie's fear made Ray feel a little—not much, but a little—better about his own. He slung the bulky sack of straw over his shoulder Santa Claus fashion and said, "Better not. If you get behind this sack, you won't be able to see the light at all."

From a few yards in, Delly turned the light back toward them. "You coming?"

"Look, Bon," Ray said. "I can carry this thing one-handed. Why not just give me the bucket and you stay out here?"

Something in his tone made Bonnie laugh. The sharp, pinched look relaxed. "You sound like you're studying to be Mother Hen Junior," she quipped, whisking in ahead of him.

The mine really had left off being damp and chill. Instead, the air was warm and sweet—not the sweetness of the time Ray had come to gather up the pieces of the serpent, but another, familiar and elusive. The source, as with the cold and heat, seemed to be in the portion of the mine nearest the stone serpent's broken hoop.

Ahead, the wagon's wheels *skreek*ed more and more slowly. Even so, Ray fell further and further behind the light. His head whirled in a jumble of unnerving images. . . . *And at center for Apple Lock, Ray Siler, the main reason this team looks like a sure bet for the Class B state championship. It's Apple Lock's ball! Gowins slips under Hancock's guard and snaps the ball to Siler, and—it's in!*

And then the sweet, sweaty-clean smell of bodies and fresh-waxed floor was gone, and there was nothing but a sense of vast well-being. . . . *The pizzas are on me! Who wants what to drink? Well, make up your mind. Look, I'm LOADED. That's right, two cheeses, two pepperonis, and one with everything. . . . And Aura Lee . . . Look, it was wrong of me to think I could take your ma's place with you. Just you come home to stay, and I swear I won't boss you around like you was one of the little ones. Why, your dad's missed you like anything, and Joe and Alva, they cried their eyes out every night the whole first week you was gone. Family's what matters . . .*

But at that the spell snapped. It had gone too far, pushed too hard, so that Ray waked to the bewildering knowledge that none of the old aches hurt any more. The darkness of Tûl Isgrun built on bitter feelings and thwarted desires, and his had evaporated. He shook himself like a dog coming out of deep water and ran for the light ahead.

Delly was working doggedly, moving as if every step took an enormous effort. He shoveled coal dust around the ramshackle pyramid of wood and straw. Bonnie held the flashlight, and though it did not waver from Delly's work, the light shimmered nervously. For a moment the two of them looked at Ray as if they had never seen him before.

"It was putting things in my head," he said awkwardly.

"Promises?" Delly drew a deep breath. "It's easier to shut out the cold and dark than promises. It surely does know how to pick a sore spot—like having Up Top shut away safe as Eden. What I can't figure is why it let up."

"Mebbe because we know it can't give what it promises." Bonnie's voice was bleak. But what it had promised her, she would not say. "C'mon, let's have another try at this old lantern."

Ray held the base and lifted the chimney while Delly struck the match—with no more success than before. Twice he dropped the match, and twice his hand jerked away before he could touch the flame to the wick. "It'd be easier if it was propane or a Coleman," Ray grumbled.

"Well, it isn't," Delly said shortly. "And I don't mean to hang around in here to find out what that thing's going to set on us next. Until it's sealed up proper, it's not going to stop trying for a handle. Here, load them two back on the wagon." He indicated the gasoline tins. The kerosene he proceeded to pour over the bonfire heap and along the coal face. Then, with Ray pulling the wagon and Bonnie on the other side with the light, he opened and tipped a gasoline can against the rear of the wagon so that they left a splashy trail behind.

Coming up the slope to the outer cave, the second can was almost emptied. Delly dribbled the last bit out carefully, bringing it to the threshold of the cave. Then, rummaging among the mining tools, he found the metal spark-maker.

"Just in case," he muttered. "You two get along Up Top, or once I get this lit I'll be running right over you."

They didn't argue.

Ray was halfway up the trail, and Bonnie not far behind, when a crashing in the brush below made them turn to see a scratched and tattered Arbie Moar scrambling along the face of the hill. As Bonnie turned and plunged downward, Mr. Moar scuttered into the hill like a wild animal going to earth.

Afterward

"Don't you go gettin' him all stirred up, now," warned Aunt Mavee. "The longer he stays flat on his stummick, the faster that back's goin' to heal." But when Ray and Bonnie opened the door of the Dreegos' spare bedroom, Delly was already up, leaning with his hands on the windowsill, watching down the Hollow. He turned eagerly.

"It's about time! Aunt Mavee won't tell me a thing, just says, 'Now don't you fret yourself' and 'Everything's goin' t' work out just fine.' Like to drive me up the wall! I don't even know what day it is. How's Arbie Moar? And how'd we get out of the Hole?"

"To start with, it's Saturday." Ray grinned. "What's that smell?" The odor was unmistakable.

Delly laughed ruefully. "Aunt Mavee's salve. It ain't half bad once you get used to it, and it must work. I sure don't feel a thing." He touched the back of his head and neck gingerly where they were bandaged.

"Hadn't you ought to be in bed?" Bonnie ventured. "The doctor said you were in shock, and when you come out you ought to take things slow and easy."

Delly's eyebrows shot up. "Aunt Mavee let a doctor at me?"

"I—we made her," Bonnie answered. "No sense taking chances."

Delly looked at her searchingly. "You don't look just right yourself."

Bonnie, touching her head-scarf self-consciously, grinned sheepishly. "I've got to pick me a new hairdo. The old one got singed half off." Her eyebrows and eyelashes were gone too, and without her usual makeup, she looked little older than Ray. Delly frowned at the blisters on her wrists and forearms and looked at her sharply.

"What *did* happen in there? All I remember is the fire not starting, and Arbie Moar roaring in like a wild man. He snatched up a pick and went down the Hole in the pitch dark. By the time I got in, he'd scattered the fire-heap. It was like he knew about it, like that was why he'd been drawn there. Then he took after me."

Ray frowned. "Then how'd the fire get started?"

"Only way it could. By accident. Arbie, he swung at

me when I was down, and the pick sparked off a rock instead. With the gas we spilled, that's all it took."

Bonnie shivered. "You had to've dragged him most of the way out. I found the both of you down that ramp, and you had him by the collar. I couldn't hardly pry you loose."

Delly shook his head wonderingly. "He wouldn't come. He fought to stay, so I had to hit him pretty hard." He pulled the bedside chair to him and gingerly sat down astride it.

"Bon had you clear up by the time I got there," Ray said. "And Mr. Moar too, almost. We'd hardly got the both of you outside when the whole thing exploded. Man, it brought Uncle Dream kiting up the Hollow ten times faster'n I thought he could ever move."

"The sheriff *did* let them right out, then. But what about Arbie?"

"He's in the hospital down in Taggert," Bonnie explained. "I been helping Jessie at the store, and she says he's still off his head. She's getting some big doctor down from Pittsburgh, but even if Arbie comes around, he'll be out of things for a good long while." She smiled. "That Jessie, she's something. Used to be she couldn't say boo to a mouse, but now she spends half the day on the telephone, ordering folks to do this and that. Those earth-movers that went up Horse Hollow? She pulled them out first thing. She says Deep Run's not going to do any more stripping or auguring in the ridges. Horse'll be a drift mine, and then go deep when the top seam's worked out. She says now she knows she's rich, she means to enjoy it, and you can't do that if all you think about is getting richer still. Besides, this way she'll get more coal out in the long run." Bonnie's eyes crinkled. "But if Arbie comes right in the head, it's gonna send him *wild.*"

Delly snorted. "He was wild enough when he come at me. How'd he slip into the Hollow anyhow, with Faye watching?"

"He came from somewheres north along the ridge," Ray said. "Uncle Dream thinks he must have clumb along Straight-Up Creek and over the top that way."

"Then he really was crazy," Delly said. "That's a mean climb even if you're fit, and the woods along up there are matted full of greenbriers. It's no wonder he was so wild and raggedy-looking." He paused a moment and looked sharply from Ray to Bonnie. "Nobody said what Jessie means to do about Twillys' Green. What happens to us?"

It might have been the way he put it, but a funny look came into Bonnie's eyes at that, and she went to the side window to stare out through the beeches. Ray shifted uncomfortably. For days Bonnie had walked around in a cloud of gloom, and now, just as she seemed to have come out of it, something set her off again. Maybe she'd got that ticket for Nashville and couldn't work herself up to say so.

"Everything's O.K.," Ray assured Delly hastily. "Even the fire in the mine, Uncle Dream says, now the vents are closed up." What if she really were leaving and came out with it right then and there? Why he should care, he didn't know; but he did. She *couldn't* go! "Th-that lawyer you saw up in Williamson? He nosed around down in Taggert and found out it was all a fake: that deed to the mineral rights, even the stuff in Aunt Neva's will."

Delly slued the chair around. "How could the *will* be a fake? What about all that stuff that was supposed to be under the floorboards in her bedroom down at Ad's?"

Bonnie opened the sack she had brought. "It was there all right. This here's what she left me. But we ought to've caught on about the will, because the one you saw was done on a typewriter. The J.P. *was* old Verl Putz, and you know he didn't take no typewriter up to church service. Aunt Neva, she signed what he wrote out by hand for her, and then old Verl goes down along and does it up with that bit about the land, and copies the way she signed. They found the first one he wrote out still in his desk. Here, lookit this." She held up a flat, silver case about five inches by nine, perhaps an inch thick. "It's real pretty, but all it's got in it is a wad of old papers."

"*Papers?*" both Ray and Delly exclaimed. Delly's hand shot out. "Let's see."

Bonnie, bewildered at their excitement, handed it over, and Delly scooted his chair back to the bed so that the others could sit on its edge and see. The case, engraved with the familiar squares and circles and squiggles of the books in the Gare, was fashioned like a large, flat capsule. The top pulled off easily, revealing a number of folded pages. Spread out on the bed, they proved to be the missing Lillico translation and several coarse vellum sheets, closely written in the strange, unreadable letters.

Delly told Bonnie about the books—incredible, Ray thought, that she had never climbed the Gare—and she was fascinated.

But when they had leafed through the pages, they were little the wiser. Rys, the man whose writings Lillico had translated, had either pieced together the tale of Tûl Isgrun from chance fragments, or worked from a source whose knowledge was little deeper than their own. There was an account of the sealing of an evil thing beneath the Dark Shrine where it had once been worshipped, and of how, having been freed long afterward, it was set up and worshipped as an oracle on Inas Ebhélic, an island where even older legends said the Ancient Ones, its enemies, had lived. When that shrine too was broken, it made its way back to Tûl Isgrun, not thinking there would be Watchers left to bind it once again.

"I wonder . . ." Delly turned the vellum pages. "Maybe these are what the Latin comes from. This map here's set in the middle of a paragraph just like in the other."

There was a sketchy little map on one of Lillico's pages, and Ray remembered the stylized one in the Latin book; but this was different. It was not as readily recognizable as Up Top as the others were—for one thing, trees were indicated on the ridges where the bogs were—but it was far more detailed. Most striking was the way the high, shallow valley was drawn as an almost perfect circle. "Makes it look sort of like a volcano," Delly observed idly.

"I'll bet it *was*," said Ray, startled. "No, really. That lawyer-guy got the geologists' reports from Mrs. Moar, and it turns out they told Arbie there wasn't likely any coal back this way at all. Somewhere along the south side of Moon Hollow they ran into—what was it?"

"Volcanic *extroo*sions," Bonnie said carefully.

"That's it. Anyhow, they say the Geological Survey only mapped this corner of the county from the air, so nobody knows for sure what it's built of. Why *couldn't* it be an old, worn-down volcano?"

Delly nodded, his mind still on the pages before him. "You know, if they all of them *do* say the same thing, there ought to be a way to figure out this writing here."

"I kind of think it's more complicated than that," Ray said diplomatically, remembering how he had fared with the Latin.

Delly smiled as he returned the sheets to their case. "It's just all them books up there. I itch to read 'em. Anyhow, it's worth a try sometime, if Bon don't mind my having the papers a while."

Bonnie jumped. "Who? Me? Oh! No, it's O.K. with me. It's just a fluke they come to me anyhow."

"Maybe." Delly seemed to take note of her preoccupation for the first time. He said, slowly, "Maybe I'll leave it for later on. What I'd really like, if you could sweet-talk Aunt Mavee into giving back the jeans Ma brought up, is take a walk up over to the old Mattick place. I've been thinking I could maybe make a stab at fixing it up, maybe live there some day."

Alarmed, Bonnie protested. "No! You mustn't do that. I mean," she faltered, "not till you're healed up. Burns, they get infected real easy."

"That's not what you meant. Look, Bon, what *is* it?"

Bonnie looked down at her hands and mumbled, "I just don't want you to get hurt makin' plans like that. Somebody's got to tell you." She sniffled. "I just didn't want it to be me."

Delly looked suddenly apprehensive. "Tell me what?" he demanded, pulling up her chin so that she was forced to look at him.

"It's Sue Ellen," Bonnie wailed, pulling away. "Her and Bob Maclehose are getting married and taking Sweet William off down to Taggert to live."

Delly sat back, still puzzled. "Well, that's a load off my mind, but why's it got you all steamed up?"

Bonnie stared at him, thunderstruck. "But—I thought —didn't *you* ask her?"

Delly grinned delightedly, but when he saw the desperate confusion on Bonnie's pretty face, he sobered quickly. "Honest, it wasn't for me. It was for Frank. Sue Ellen, she can hardly look out for herself, and when that kid grows past being dressed up and cuddled, she's going to be purely at a loss. Me and Frank was so close —well, I owed him. But you got to understand—" He took Bonnie's hands in his own. "I was done for the day I went off to the army. The last thing I seen of the Hollow was you up a tree, whistle-singing to some bird, and . . ."

Ray, very belatedly, realized that what he was listening in on wasn't just comfortable family gossip. Bonnie was looking as if she might float straight up to the ceiling if she hadn't been held down.

He bolted for the door.

Home to Stay

Uncle Dream, coming up the steps, could not understand why he ought to turn around and go right down again. "Delly's all right, ain't he?"

"Merciful heavens, Dream!" Below, Aunt Mavee laughed. "Come along down. I suspect your boy Ray there's not lost his wits so much as those two upstairs have found theirs. About time, too!"

"Well, I'll *be*. . . !" was all Dream could say.

Later, when they had gone up across the fields and looked down across the ragged beauty of the neglected valley, Ray repeated Delly's remark about fixing up the old Mattick place. "Did he, now?" Uncle Dream thrust his hands deep in his overall pockets. "S'funny. Harry 'n Ad 'n me been talking about that ourselves."

Ray, in his excitement, almost danced like a little kid. "Honest? Where? Where did Grandpa live when he was up here?"

"Whoa back there!" His uncle stopped in his tracks, looking worried. "It wasn't but an idea. Roney says it's crazy. And it's true, like Cloyce says, it'd make it awful hard on the little ones, gettin' down to school. He's got that bad back, too, so him and Erla, they'd have to stay put."

"But it wouldn't be more'n ten or fifteen minutes longer to the school bus, would it?" Ray protested. "Rainelle and June Ann, they wouldn't mind."

"No. But before long there'll be Jody and then the baby. It's a stiff climb for little ones, and the old Clewarek place is a good quarter mile further'n Dreegos'." Uncle Dream waved a hand in the general direction of the western rim of the valley.

"Besides—" He looked at Ray unhappily as he dug into his pocket. "There's this. It's from your dad. Jessie give it to me yesterday and I forgot to pass it on." He held out a crumpled envelope, and as Ray took it, reluctantly, he pulled out another. "I got this one myself, three-four days back, and didn't have the heart to ask y' about it. Your daddy says you asked to come home, and he sent you a bus ticket. I was to be sure you didn't cash it in and spend the money. You didn't do that, did you, boy?"

It was not really a question. That, perhaps more than anything else, made Ray realize how quickly he had come to love his big, slow uncle. "No. I sent it back." Then, to be fair to his father, he had to add, "But he knows I might have."

Tearing open his own letter, he scanned it quickly and then held it out. It read *Good enough. Let us hear from you once in a while. Yours, Dad.* Paper-clipped to it were a twenty-five dollar savings bond in Ray's name and a check for fifteen made out to Durham Clark. *P.S.* the letter said. *Your ma bought you this bond when you were born. I came across it when we cleared her stuff out.*

Uncle Dream shook his head. "A hard man." Then he smiled. "But I guess that don't matter any more. Look, we got time, what do you say we go over and see what shape the old house is in? I don't see why we couldn't come up here summers. Might be just the thing. You can grow the sweetest melons alive up here. . . . We might even put in a bit of garden this year if we was quick about it. Seeds ought to be in up here right now."

Ray couldn't say a word. He knew he was too big to do such a thing, but here it didn't seem to matter: he slipped his hand into his uncle's as they walked along. He could not have been happier if he had been Ruan, come home at last after twice eight hundred years.